THE LEGACY SERIES

Series Titles

Self-Defense
Corey Mertes

Where Are Your People From?
James B. De Monte

Finding the Bones: Stories & A Novella
Nikki Kallio

Sometimes Creek
Steve Fox

The Plagues
Joe Baumann

The Clayfields
Elise Gregory

Kind of Blue
Christopher Chambers

Evangelina Everyday
Dawn Burns

Township
Jamie Lyn Smith

Responsible Adults
Patricia Ann McNair

Great Escapes from Detroit
Joseph O'Malley

Nothing to Lose
Kim Suhr

The Appointed Hour
Susanne Davis

Praise for
Self-Defense

"In *Self-Defense*, Corey Mertes writes stories so sure of themselves, so representative of the vastness in each seemingly ordinary life, that one wonders if these tales always existed and he simply conjured them. There's no artifice to be found here. Mertes is the real deal, not so much writing stories as he is bringing them out of hiding as though by séance."

—Jeff Vande Zande
author of *Rules of Order*

"With striking prose and exactitude, Corey Mertes's *Self-Defense* follows a collection of strange, sad, but wholly unique characters through twelve unforgettable stories, all seeking a version of self-defense against their own demons and disappointments. A gritty but emotionally sensitive clutch of tales."

—Kali White
author of *The Monsters We Make*

"In this collection, Corey Mertes takes readers on an unsentimental journey into casinos, ballroom dance studios, Los Angeles dives, and flood plains—places where hard-luck characters are always on the con, their lives a whirling vortex of bad luck and bad love. Mertes balances their grim situations with humor and a touch of empathy. While the stories rarely end well, a resilient spirit emerges. The stories themselves are as addictive as the throw of the dice or turn of the cards that Mertes' gambling addicts can't resist. This is superb writing—fresh, unsparing but never disdainful, and steeped in first-hand knowledge of the subject. Bravo."

—Pat MacEnulty
author of *The Language of Sharks* and *Time to Say Goodbye*

"In clubs and casinos—in overgrown backyards, ballroom-dance studios, and down-and-out motels—the characters in Corey Mertes's debut collection desperately try to defend themselves against the lure of drugs and booze and the scourges of illness and infidelity. *Self-Defense* may be full of failed dreams, but it is charged with memorable characters, whip-smart dialogue, and bleak landscapes rendered beautiful by the author's lyrical prose."

—Rita Ciresi
author of *Pink Slip* and *Sometimes I Dream in Italian*

"Mertes' stories pull no punches. The characters in *Self-Defense* have spent years instigating their own battles and blocking their own shots. In clear, uncompromising language, Mertes places his characters' cards face up on the table and refuses to deal them new ones. These stories crackle with unfulfilled longing."

—Julie Babcock
author of *Rules for Rearrangement*

"*Self-Defense* is more than a collection of short stories. It is a captivating peek into the heart, joy, and sadness of a brilliant storyteller. Each story is masterfully written on several levels. Mertes will make you smile, touch your heart, and cause you to reflect on your mortality. I read the collection in one sitting and, two days later, reread it. *Self-Defense* will be a book you recommend to your friends, but keep it handy, for you will return to its extraordinary stories often. Five stars, hands down. Bravo."

—Nick Chiarkas
author of *Weepers* and *Nunzio's Way*

"*Self-Defense* is so hardboiled that Raymond Chandler would chip a tooth on it. Time and again, in casinos, on oil rigs, dance floors, and film sets, men and women who are down on their luck roll the dice and take their chances."

—Scott Dominic Carpenter
author of *This Jealous Earth* and *French Like Moi*

Self-Defense

Stories

Corey Mertes

Cornerstone Press
Stevens Point, Wisconsin

Cornerstone Press, Stevens Point, Wisconsin 54481
Copyright © 2023 Corey Mertes
www.uwsp.edu/cornerstone

Printed in the United States of America by
Point Print and Design Studio, Stevens Point, Wisconsin

Library of Congress Control Number: 2022948940
ISBN: 979-8-9869663-4-2

Cornerstone Press titles are produced in courses and internships offered by the Department of English at the University of Wisconsin–Stevens Point.

DIRECTOR & PUBLISHER   EXECUTIVE EDITOR
Dr. Ross K. Tangedal   Jeff Snowbarger

SENIOR EDITORS
Lexie Neeley, Monica Swinick, Kala Buttke

PRESS STAFF
Ellie Atkinson, Grace Dahl, Lauren Engelbreth, Patrick Fogarty, Angela Green, Cal Henkens, Brett Hill, Julia Kaufman, Catriona Scheinost, Maria Scherer, Taylor Schmidt, Cash Van Stiphout, Matt Vancik, Abbi Wasielewski

For Zach and Julia, naturally
and for Jen, for enduring

Stories

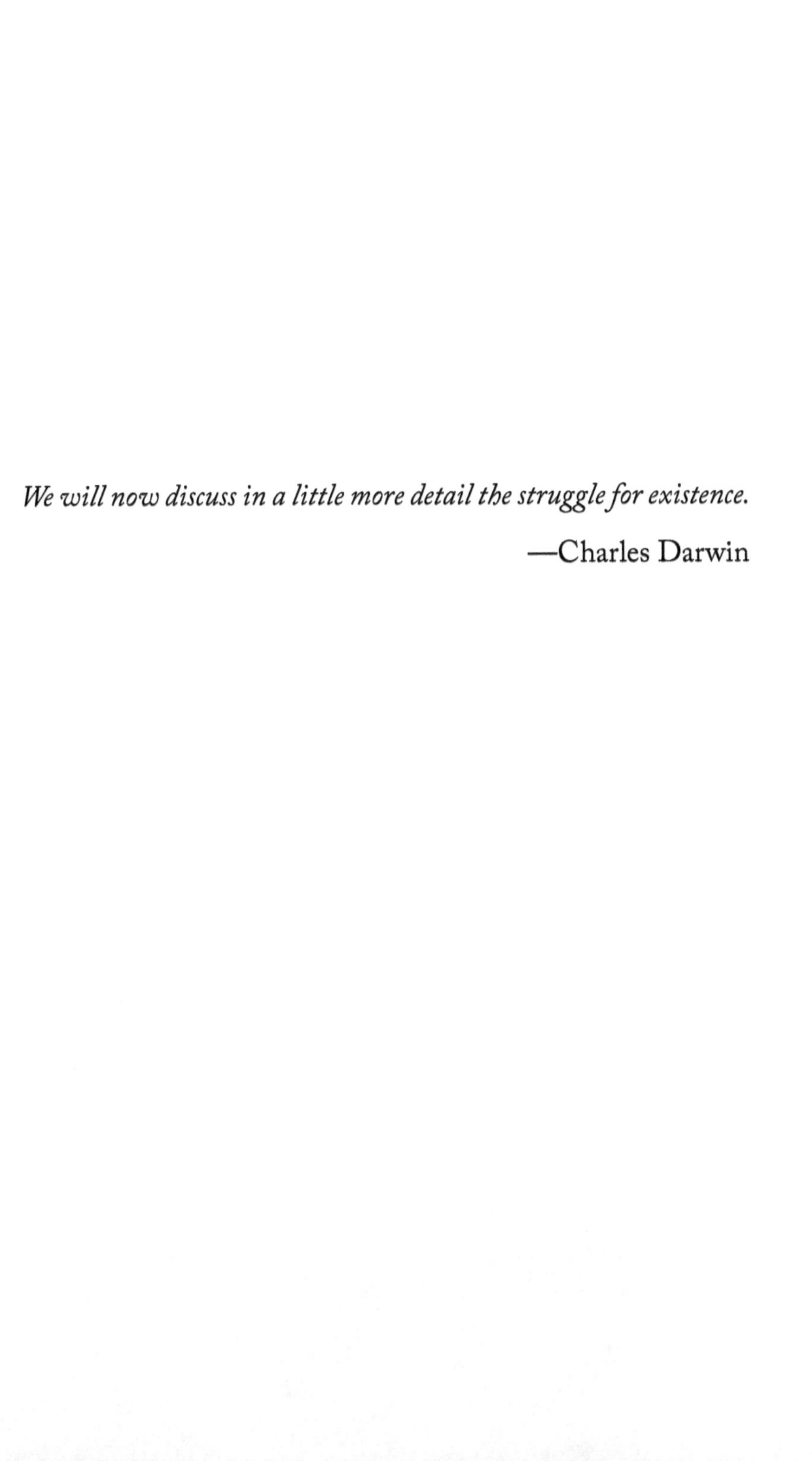

We will now discuss in a little more detail the struggle for existence.

—Charles Darwin

Rabbit

They live on opposite coasts now: the old man with his third wife in a Victorian Shingle on Cape Cod; the woman, alone, in a run-down bungalow just a few blocks from Santa Monica Beach. Many years earlier, when the woman was only a girl, they'd been neighbors. The man had lived next door to the girl and her family in an outer ring suburb of Chicago.

The man had been a successful chef at that time, having trained and worked his way up at some of the city's most celebrated restaurants. He had recently opened a restaurant of his own and the initial reviews had been favorable. Critics especially praised his inventiveness, most frequently noting the section of his tapas menu titled "For the Brave," which included such exotic fare as pig ear salad, roasted marrow bones with shallots, and duck tongue tacos. The girl was a typical ten-year-old. She went to public school. Her father was an executive at a greeting card company, and her mother worked part-time for a non-profit agency while raising the girl and her two brothers.

An incident occurred during that period involving a rabbit. It was the girl's rabbit, a female American Chinchilla, which she kept in a cage in her backyard during the spring and summer. The girl's family and the chef next door were all devoted pet owners. Her older brother owned a leopard gecko, and her younger brother kept tropical fish in a large tank in their basement. The family also owned three cats.

The chef, for his part, preferred dogs. He, along with the woman he was living with at that time, a performance artist (this was between the first and second wives and before he ever met the third, a sculptor), kept three dogs, each as exotic in its own way as the items on his menu: a Basenji, a Corgi puppy, and a very handsome, golden rust–colored Vizsla, the man's pride and joy. It was primarily for the dogs' sake, to provide them with fresh air and open space, that he lived such a long commute from his restaurant and the city life he adored.

On Mondays the restaurant was closed. Some Mondays his girlfriend cooked and they watched movies together and made love. As often as not, the couple's lovemaking incorporated toys they had purchased from a sex shop located in an adjacent suburb with less restrictive zoning. Once when his girlfriend was rehearsing in town, however, the man stayed home alone on a Monday night with the intention of catching up on his yard work, a set of chores he loathed and always put off as long as he could, sometimes even to the point where a neighbor would sneer at him or leave a nasty note in his mailbox. He put it off this night, too; so long, in fact, that it was getting dark when he finally went outside. He balanced a glass of wine and a mini-flashlight in one hand as he watered the dried-out azaleas out front with a loosely gripped hose in the other. Standing there in the dark in wet sandals and robe, he began to second-guess his own reasoning for choosing to reside in such a sleepy outpost, when suddenly he was reminded why he did by the playful bounding of his golden Vizsla around the side of the house. Only when he put down everything but the drink and was crouching over to rub the dog's head did he notice that it held something in its mouth, something fat and furry. On closer examination he saw that it was the rabbit from next door, as dead as the neighborhood.

"Jesus," the man said, as the dog dropped the rabbit at his feet. The wine glass slipped from his hand and shattered on a stone border.

He had only spoken to the neighbor girl once or twice, exchanging the briefest of pleasantries, noting only that she looked tall for her age and wore skirts that didn't fit right, but he knew immediately that it was her rabbit because he had seen her caring for it and it had a distinctive circular patch of pure white fur on its back, like a sunlit glade in a pencil-gray forest. He shone the light on the white spot. Then he shone the light through a gap in the slatted wood fence that separated the properties. Weeks earlier a storm had knocked down a section of the fence and it was agreed with the neighbor that it was the chef's responsibility to fix it. Like so many other home maintenance projects, he had put off the job. Now his neglect had apparently allowed his dog access to his neighbor's yard and, somehow, the encaged rabbit. Though barely visible, the cage was clearly empty, its door wide open, confirming what the man already knew.

His first instinct was to cover up the deed by burying the dead animal and keeping quiet. That impulse lasted longer than it might in many other men. While searching his garage for a shovel, however, conscience got the better of him, and he decided the proper course was to take the rabbit next door and explain honestly to the girl's father what had happened.

At their doorstep, he faltered. Like everywhere else, the lights there were out. It occurred to him that it might add insult to injury to awaken the family from their safe suburban dreams with a cold nocturnal lesson in Darwin. Besides, despite a secure place in the hospitality industry, the man had never been entirely comfortable talking with people. The most difficult part of his new role as restaurateur was greeting the house, which forced him to confront his lifelong awkwardness around strangers. He certainly did not relish the prospect of facing the father, or worse, confessing to the child that his own delinquency had contributed to the death of her precious ward. Might there not also be criminal charges, he wondered? Could they take away his dog? He was no expert on the law. In the end he decided that before taking any action he would store the rabbit in his garage and wait up to discuss the situation with his girlfriend, whose opinion he still valued.

It was a good choice. His girlfriend had a practical suggestion. Noticing there were no visible marks on the rabbit, she said why not just replace it in its cage while everyone is sleeping? Sure, the neighbor girl would be distraught when she found the rabbit dead in the morning, but that could hardly be avoided. Animals—and human beings, for that matter—are mortal, it's a lesson every child has to learn. God knows the woman herself had had to learn it. Why confuse the girl's emotional state by linking her loss to a seldom-seen neighbor instead of to the immutable fact that everything dies?

The man was not mindless of the self-serving end to her idea, but found that it did not detract from her reasoning, which was sound. So, at three in the morning, he slunk into the next yard, locked the dead rabbit in its enclosure, and hurried home to bed.

* * *

"The strangest thing happened the other day," the father next door was saying the following Saturday morning. He had just finished cutting his lawn, and his neighbor, the chef, was finally about to begin cutting his, but was having trouble getting the mower started. The father came over with some helpful advice that segued into a friendly chat about machines and sports and how money makes the world go round. Eventually the talk took a more personal turn.

"My daughter's rabbit died."

"Oh, I'm sorry," the man said.

"No . . . well, thank you. That's not the strange thing, of course. The rabbit was old. It died a week ago Friday. We buried it in the backyard."

Far in the distance a dog began to bark. The man caught himself counting the number of barks until they died away at eight.

"The strange thing was, a few days later it reappeared in its cage. Still dead, naturally. The cage door locked. My daughter was the first to discover it." Here the father lowered one eyebrow along with his voice, imparting upon his next words a tone of inquiry instead of goodwill.

"We still don't have an explanation for it. Maybe some kids playing a prank. My daughter was terrified, as you can imagine. She's hardly left her room since."

With that, he tipped his head back and to the left. The chef looked over his neighbor's shoulder just in time to see the girl yank the red curtains shut in a second-floor window.

* * *

That's the whole story. Not much to it, really. The man did not tell the father then, nor ever, that his dog had dug up the rabbit and that it was he, the man, who believing his dog the killer and afraid of the consequences, had covered it up by returning the animal to its cage. The girl snapped out of her self-imposed hermitage in a few days.

And yet who can say how much a narrow but intimate drama affects the lives of its players? Even a seemingly inconsequential disturbance may leave an unseen trace, invisible forensic evidence of a crime of the subconscious. No measurement has been invented like a tablespoon or a carafe to calculate the impact on our hearts and minds of a compressed and finite human sequence. That the man soon took rabbit off his menu, previously a favorite of his braised with bacon, tomato, and olives, may be a subconscious reaction to his late-night deceit or simply a reflection of the incident's most unremarkable truth: everything gets old. That he also had been known previously for his embracement of the farm-to-table movement, for using humanely raised, hormone-free rabbits and poultry, and that his emphasis on that movement began to wane shortly after the misfortune, may likewise be pointed to as a product of either the truth or the lie—or neither. In two other restaurants he subsequently owned, one in that same city, the other on the East Coast, he would periodically add a rabbit dish to his offerings but was no longer so particular about the animal's upbringing. These were invariably temporary experiments; the item was always removed within a week or two at the most, regardless of its popularity, for reasons he could not explain to his customers or himself.

The effect of the incident on the girl was more complicated and severe, perhaps because she was so much younger. Living so close now to the earth's largest ocean she will occasionally walk to the strand and skip stones at the incoming foam—forcefully, as if to disturb the natural mechanics of life's repeating currents. She never married.

Her father died in a car wreck when she was eighteen. In her youth she developed a lifelong sensitivity to evidence of hidden powers, to what individually are referred to as superstitions, astrology, the occult, magic, but which may, in their composite effect on her, be better described as a propensity to read into things. She has read into the whistle of a midnight wind, for example, the voice of a reappearing spirit. To her, the stars and the planets foretell, the palm is a predictor, accidents are not accidents at all. Into a chance encounter with a recent acquaintance, she will mistakenly read the inevitability of a mutual fate. There were times in her teenage years when she would ask herself and God what portion of who she is, if any, she could trace directly to the circumstances concerning, for instance, the rabbit. The same question put later became to what extent each wave transforms the timeless sea or is altered by the skipping of a stone. The only answer she ever receives is the melancholy approach of an indivisible tide.

And so it is with the old man but in reverse, a continent away. His wife, who is much younger than he is, cares for him now as his body diminishes: not a piece at a time, a process he could understand and explain, but in a gradual reduction of the whole, like a desiccating fruit. In his home on the Cape, he will sit with a blanket on his lap and watch game shows or stare out the window. He is also experiencing the first flashes of dementia. His mind is like a game of Wheel of Fortune on slow rewind in which one at a time the letters of his life are hidden from him rather than revealed.

Outside he may see a young girl walking home with a boy from her middle school class. He has seen it. He has seen them stop and kiss at the corner from which they go their separate ways home, seen the boy caress a loose strand of her hair and run off, leaving the girl aglow with the magic of her own and the world's potential. Once after just such a kiss she saw the old man watching from his bedroom window. She was not embarrassed. She put a finger to her lips as if to secure his confidence, and he nodded in agreement. Later, when the dementia was worse, he would see the girl on the street or in her yard when he went on his walks and she would smile at him and wink, reaffirming their little secret. He would wink too but did not remember what the secret was or even that they had one. Instead, he wondered if the girl, flirtatious as she was, was much older than he imagined, and why the sight of her seemed to arouse him from a deep sleep, and why it always made him think about rabbit.

Violins

The man standing next to me starts talking. It's some prattle about the music industry's passing inspired by the track he's been listening to through giant earphones and taking notes about on his iPad. He claims some connection with Los Angeles.

"...As soon as I can raise the money I'm going back."

The bar at the Rialto is a teak simulacrum of an idealized woman's body. The order he barks at his service dog is in another language. I guess German because the dog looks like a German shepherd, but I am wildly off base. It's some hybrid of Portuguese and Spanish, he says, the name of which I do not recognize. Is he putting me on? How stupid do I look?

"Why a service dog?" I inquire grudgingly.

I doubt he'll be offended. He isn't blind. No obvious disability. It's like he doesn't hear me when instead of answering he says he's back in town to capitalize on the fledgling medical marijuana industry as a cultivator. That's probably a lie. It's obvious I'm stoned. His teeth are a jagged mess, a coral reef. He's living at the American Inn, if you could call that living. The next day in bed he calls me Candy, so I steal a few bucks from his wallet while he's taking a shower. His name is Adam, according to his expired license. Add him to the list.

* * *

I am not always this much of a skank. Ironically, it happens after those rare moments of self-preservation. A night earlier my old man demolished his Fender on the mantelpiece and made a point of announcing it to the uninitiated neighbors.

"She wants me to give up my music?" he yelled at a wary jogger.

"I didn't say that," doing my best to remain calm.

"She wants me to get more serious about money?" he asked the bewildered boy on the stoop. "Fine! I give it up!"

"I didn't say that."

"What!" He turned and bumped his head on the window frame.

"I said I didn't say that," I chuckled. "Oh, fuck it." I marched out with a duffel bag full of underwear and all the hanging clothes I could grab in one bear hug, and then holed up in the back room of my shop until further notice.

After Adam, and before the new tattoo, came a stunned college student I shared a spliff with in the Knuckleheads alley, and a married executive in health care technology named Noah, who came into the oddities shop alone and kept peeking my way while caressing the miniature skulls. I approached the executive hips first.

"Can I interest you in a little head?" I said, subtly. He screwed like it was his first affair since the Flood and offered me cash on the way out.

"Ha ha," I responded, but still gave him my real number.

* * *

Zipper at Old Souls knew his customers; he used to sell cars. "Cola! You only come by after a breakup."

"Not yet, but soon." I popped a red jellybean from the bowl by the register. "This one'll be a lulu."

"What's it gonna be, Disney or fright film?"

He knew my left arm and shoulder were set aside for divine Walt's pre-Monster creations: Coal-haired Pocahontas paddling up-vein. Illusive Mulan posing as warrior along a sinewy bicep. Nala splayed crudely across a buff delt. On the right, manifestations of moviedom horror from Pinhead and Pennywise to Jason Voorhees and Jack Torrance.

"I want something new," I said, flipping open the catalogue. When I described my explosive relationship, he pointed at TNT with a banner that read "Ka-boom!" Not so big on ideas, old Zip, but he could draw like Ingres. Something must have stuck, because I settled on a caduceus with the staff running up my sternum surmounted by clavicular wings, and winding along one snake a postscript directed at my soon-to-be ex that read "Not your boo."

As I'd assured Zipper, the split, when it came, was a doozy. When I arrived for my stuff, my man-child was strumming on a seldom-played banjo, an instrument he'd inherited and detested, but the only one still left undamaged. On mute in the background played one of the cop shows he liked from the 1970s. In the Age of Content, he had found a platform that streams nothing but obsolete crap. Kojak sucking on a lollipop, Mannix getting his man. Or was that Baretta? I never could keep them straight. Maybe Kojak sucking on a Beretta. The first night we had sex we'd watched Weekend Update on an *SNL* episode with the original cast. He loved the dowdy editorialist, Emily Litella.

I'm here tonight to speak out against busting school children. Imagine, busting school children! The food in jail isn't good.

"You get it?" he'd asked. "It should be *busing*, not *busting*."

"Yeah, yeah. She's old so she mistakes one thing for another."

Comedy ages like dogs: fifteen years is a lifetime. Forty-five and you might as well be wearing blackface or burning cats. You wouldn't know it from watching him, though. He would laugh out loud when Archie Bunker called his wife a dingbat or when Ruth Buzzi purse-whipped that bespectacled old pervert on *Laugh-In*. Oh, I tried to go along in the beginning. But over time that effort became more contrived than an episode of *Charlie's Angels*.

What's all this I keep hearing about five crustaceans hijacking an airplane?

"Okay. Croatians, right?" I'd ask half-heartedly, by that point aware that the age difference was a bigger obstacle than we could ever laugh off.

"I think so," he'd say gloomily, no doubt beginning to reach the same conclusion.

I could have written the script for what happened next. He followed me into the bedroom.

"Where do you think you're going?"

"I think we've had enough, don't you?"

"I'll say when we've had enough."

I'll say when we've had enough. Where do you think you're going? He knew all the clichés. No wonder his lyrics stank.

"You're making a big mistake." He laid the banjo on the bed. Two crushed beer cans for eyes made it look like a deviant smile. From the closet I pulled the portmanteau with the blue velvet interior I'd purchased at auction with the intention of reselling in the shop, and started packing.

"You knew what you were getting into," he said. "The good with the bad."

"What's the good again? Remind me."

He reached for my arm. I pulled back and positioned my hands in a sideways T, as I'd been taught in Self-Defense.

"Easy," he said. "I am not the Monster."

"No, but you would've gotten along."

From there followed a predictable dance. Knee-jerk defenses. Tirades like arias. One step forward, two steps back. Ending with wall knocks from an exasperated neighbor and a spontaneous response in two-part harmony: "Mind your own *fucking* business!"

I'd deliberately worn a button-down shirt and no bra in case he gave me an opening for a Big Reveal. When he said, "You're no good for anybody else, baby, remember that," I tore the shirt open. Buttons popped like lottery balls. At first, he looked confused, like a child who's been offered a candy bar in the middle of a spanking. He took a step forward before I pointed at the snake.

"Oh, funny," he said, reading my tender goodbye. His cupped hands drooped to the side. "You'd fuck up your body for one stupid joke."

"Yeah, well, I'm no Gilda Radner."

"You're damn right."

"'The medium is the message,'" I said, changing into a tank top. "To borrow a line from your generation, *baby*."

"Marvelous. You're putting that art school education to good use." His blind reach for the inlaid case on the mantle resulted in a scattering of weed. "Son of a bitch." Bent over, he added, "I'm not *that* old, by the way."

"You could've fooled me."

Flaps of unfolded clothing stuck out from the edges of the suitcase as I pressed it shut.

"I'll come back for the television," I said on the way out.

"This one?"

When I turned, he was tipping it from the shelf. The screen burst on the hardwood like scattering bats. I made it out the door. He clawed Freddy Krueger on the landing. I whip-spun and caught him in rib #6 with The Little Mermaid, then thrust into his chin with the base of my palm.

What's all this fuss I keep hearing about violins on television?

He rolled down the stairs like the boulder of Sisyphus. The bulky trunk bounced off each step like clock strikes, then into his curled-up body with a time-ending thud.

"On second thought, you can keep the TV."

He groaned the French alphabet. Blood from his ear formed a scarlet brook. The pig in 1C screamed that she'd called the police; already you could hear the sirens. I spat at her feet as she waddled back inside.

None of this makes me out to be very sympathetic. Dr. Krantz, with her usual understatement, says that sympathy is an emotion whose virtues I have not had credibly confirmed. What I felt instead was envy, as from my car I watched two cute paramedics fasten my ex to a stretcher. Envy because they knew who they were, because *he* knew, for a change, at least for the immediate future, exactly where he was going.

"Wait!" I called out as they were shutting the doors.

"That's her. That's the bitch!"

I ran up the stairs and passed two policemen on the way down. They allowed me to go by but then stopped me at the ambulance doors.

"He just hates to go anywhere without his banjo," I said, smiling brightly, holding it up as though evidence of my good faith.

"Do you know the victim?" asked the taller one with the Roman nose. He couldn't have been more than one year out of the academy.

"He *was* my boo," I said, with an involuntary wink.

In the end, he recovered and didn't press charges. The tall young cop took my statement at the precinct, where I sat with my trunk between my legs and looked for patterns in the grime on the barren gray walls.

"Name?"

"Cola. Like the soft drink. Lefebvre. It's spelled—"

"Address?"

Two raucous teenagers wearing handcuffs were escorted in roughly by a fat sergeant with a bulbous nose. At the front desk, one of them called him "porky" and the other one laughed. The sergeant hauled them into a vacant office where he beat the crap out of them both. One and then the other, you could see the shadowy smudge of their faces pressed against the frosted glass and hear their muffled cries. They sounded like wild animals. Even in pain they remained defiant. I have to admit it turned me on more than just a little. For the first time I became conscious of why someone like my ex, or like myself for that matter, would cling to the stale signposts of childhood, from the one time in life when he, or I, in the absence of interference, might have walked the earth like tigers, full of power and courage and brio.

"*Address?*"

"Precinct 69. Until I can come up with something better."

We were in Precinct 12. I thought it was funny. He entered what I said without smiling, kind of proving my point about comedy.

Several years later, with a different doctor, I mentioned a recurring dream I'd been having.

"Do you want me to tell you about it?"

"If you like."

He lit a cigarette but didn't offer me one.

"I thought therapists only smoked pipes."

"Hmm."

I described myself wearing a pink taffeta dress and a tiara walking down a hall with many doors, all of which were oblong or trapezoidal or distorted in some other way, and approaching each from Dutch angles like in a funhouse or *The Third Man*. From behind one of them I heard chamber music, either Mozart or Vivaldi. I banged on the door with my fists. I was desperate to get in, yelling, pleading, crying for help, until finally it opened. Inside: a string quartet. Four middle-aged men with instruments seated on wooden chairs, every one of them buck naked. They stopped playing and turned in my direction. "I told them I must have the wrong room. And then I woke up."

"Ah."

He rolled the cigarette between his fingers and studied it like it was a pen and he was a meticulous scribe. Outside, roosting birds fled the protection of a rambling oak, storm clouds mounted behind distant towers.

"Well?"

"Well what?"

I had a sudden urge to crack open his skull with the globular paperweight on his desk or put that cigarette out in his eye.

"What do you think it means?"

He turned a dial on his fancy watch.

"How do I know?" he said, brushing away a fly. "It's your dream."

Hollywood

I was renting a small space in Hollywood back then across the hall from an alcoholic named Mike 109. The manager occupied the apartment next door. He smoked continuously and kept old racing forms stacked up in his living room chest high. Sometimes outside my window at night a woman dressed in pink mohair, known for plastering her image on billboards all over town, would sell her time, or body, or drugs to the kind of men to whom pink and false fame were alluring.

These are not the people I want to tell you about. The first one I met on the street on the way to my car. It was winter, although you would never know it. The sun gave no indication that it was coming or going. An acquaintance at the acting class I could no longer afford had loaned me his expired ID from UCLA so that I could use the campus weight room without paying. Five years earlier, in Milwaukee, I'd been greedily misled by the praise I won for my portrayal of Dr. Einstein in a high school production of *Arsenic and Old Lace*. Stacy Kramer was the name the guy gave when he pulled up alongside me and asked for directions.

We struck up a conversation: the weather back home, the price of tea in Kirkuk. I was wearing black shorts and high-tops with no shirt. His convertible Mercedes glistened in the shimmering light.

—Nice car, I said.

He never looked me in the eye. Glasses, thinning hair, a spare tire. Talk, talk, talk.

—Say, he said. You feel like going to a party tonight? He pulled out a photograph from his wallet.

—Well, that depends.

The picture was of him in a suit, all smiles, in front of the Shrine Auditorium, his arms around two women half his age. I recognized the one in the red dress, an actress known at the time for her role in a popular sitcom, the timer still ticking down on her fifteen minutes of fame.

—She's the one throwing it, he said, and gave me a thumbs up. Lots of girls, believe me.

Who was I to doubt? *What* was I? Serving process one week, selling Amway another. Unread books on my bed about how to flip houses. In today's world it might be Uber Eats or recycled merchandise on eBay.

—Sure, I said, all nonchalant. I like girls.

We met up on the patio of the Hotel Bel Air to juice up, as he put it, before the party. You should see this place. Cocooned in a forest of ficus and palms. Spanish tile roofs, exterior walls the color of babies' skin. A sultan would turn red. A perfect oval pool so secluded and serene it might have been filled with amniotic fluid.

—Thank *you*, Mr. Kramer, the maître d' said when the guy slipped him a twenty-dollar bill.

They bowed to him there like he was the King of Freedonia. He was greeted the same way at our next stops, the Four Seasons and the Beverly Hilton. Madonna walked into the latter, incognito beneath a headscarf and sunglasses, betrayed by her ultra-chic entourage.

—I do hotels, the guy said. That's what *I* do. Not that he ever asked me. At each hotel he ordered the rounds for us both.

—You don't get a beer in a place like this, he said at the Hilton, having told the waiter, with a little wink, to bring two Purple Rose of Cairos *the way I like them*. By the third drink I couldn't remember his name, or mine. From what I could gather he had a permanent suite there, which he assured me would be our last stop before moving on to the party.

—You don't have any weed, do you? I asked, although I didn't want or need any.

—Never touch the stuff, he assured me. I came into this world clear-eyed. No illusions. Started with nothing and now look. I built seven hotels right here in Southern California. For emphasis he jabbed his middle finger into the mosaic table.

—Who did I know? he continued. Nobody, that's who. Today I've got Ted Danson in my book. Joan Cusack, Annie Lennox. The mayor will take my call at four in the morning. Clear-eyed, he repeated, scissor-pointing at his eyes. And that's how I intend to keep it.

He sipped his drink and surveyed my posture. My facial reaction, for I hadn't said much to that point, must have betrayed my indifference masquerading as doubt—or vice versa, it's so long ago now—because he withdrew more photographs from his satchel to prove his point. Here he was shaking hands with David Bowie, there alongside Nancy Reagan at some fundraiser. Oh, and look, a lavish event for the rich outside the Magic Castle—and, remembering the pretext for our evening festivities, images from gala openings with fashionable young women, including half a dozen more with the actress hosting the alleged party that night somewhere deep in the dark, lonesome Valley.

Things went the same way during one last drink in his suite. We did a few lines, clear-eyed to the end. I was beginning to figure things out. More photographs were presented, an entire album, just prior to his exit from the bathroom with a too-casual offer of a Swedish massage, the type at which he assured me the actress's sexy friend would later prove she was an expert. The main event took place a short time later in the hall. Me shifting my weight, punching the elevator button in short jabs; him and his hairy belly pleading from the doorway, wearing nothing but black socks and boxer shorts decorated with colorful safari animals.

It's the silent yearning that tolls the heart's decline. I did wind up meeting a couple movie stars that night, a young man and woman, whose names I feel obligated to withhold. I had decided to sober up by shooting pool at the Quism Room. The young man happened to be shooting on the table next to me, by himself.

—You shoot good, mister, I lied, playing it cool. I thought that, being a movie actor, he might recognize the line from *The Hustler*, but it didn't seem to register.

—Thanks.

—Wanna play?

—I'm waiting for someone, but okay. Until she gets here.

I could tell right away he was an asshole. Under different circumstances, we might have been friends.

—You break.

We shot a few games before his girlfriend arrived. I had a feeling it would be her. I knew about their romance from the tabloids. She was a lot more famous than he was. They kissed on the lips for a long time, like it really meant something.

—This is J—, he said finally, to be polite.

—Hi.

—I saw that film you were in about the high school, I said.

—You did? Okay.

—I wanted to fuck you ever since.

—Oh God.

The boyfriend's jaw tightened. He dropped his arms and took a step forward, although the long table stood firmly between us.

—What did you say?

—Shootin' it up here, boss. I bent over and banked the twelve. The woman put a hand to his chest.

—It's not worth it, she said.

—You're a prick, you know that buddy. He'd raised his voice. Everyone else in the room—they were all middle-aged men—for a second time stopped what they were doing, the first time having been when the woman initially walked in and crossed over to us, with her legs like Greek columns. These men, all dreams and false swagger, were on my side without knowing it, even if, or maybe because, the other guy was vaguely recognizable.

—I haven't seen any of *your* movies, I said. Six in the side.

The couple did not want to make the papers so they left. The thought of their sumptuous evening ahead, tarnished by the effect of my insult, made me smile.

From there I could walk to my favorite bar along Hollywood Boulevard. Over hardened handprints I recited passages from *A Streetcar Named Desire* longing for an unnamable justice. A star near the horizon sparkled like a diamond stud in the celestial sphere. Near the front door I stumbled atop a tribute to a silent film actress on which a week earlier my companion for that night, a biker, who when we first met and I asked him the time revealed a wristwatch tattoo set to 4:20, had taken a prolonged piss.

Though it was late, a vendor still manned a street-lit kiosk selling sports memorabilia. He called every patron and passerby *cuz*. I paused for a smoke on a nearby bench.

—Naw, naw, cuz, he was saying to some tourist seeking Dodgers collectibles. You want that shit, go to the Stadium. I'll sell you a map.

What he was peddling instead was unique: t-shirts and pennants, not of winning teams, but of those that had lost in the championship. Limited edition merchandise pre-ordered by the runners-up with the intention of wearing on the platform if they had won. I purchased a cap that falsely proclaimed the Brewers the winners of the '82 World Series. My cousin and I shared stories about bitter endings and the dreams of wandering fools.

—Vaya con Dios, he said, when finally I pressed my way into the bar. Something something God.

Inside, the contrast between the mural of Hollywood legends on the wall and the lushes and misfits colonizing the stools made a credible case for eugenics. The jukebox pretended to be Marianne Faithfull. One of the bartenders was a guy with a beard wearing a calico dress.

I settled in beside a tall woman with a ring through her nose and a tattoo of a serpent down her bony bare leg. Her black hair, or wig, more than likely, framed her pale face in the shape of a proscenium.

—Let's get out of here, I said, after ordering a beer.

—Go to hell.

She had one tooth missing and a disproportionately long middle finger. From the next room I could hear the tapping and testing of a finicky mic. I had forgotten that Thursdays were poetry nights. Seats were set up before a makeshift stage. One beer later my spirited companion recited a piece from a folded paper she pulled out of her bra, and from her gypsy soul.

> *. . . She escapes to a place where pain is a barometer*
> *and pressure is the pressure of a complete person*
> *who may not care about basketball*
> *and may laugh two seconds before each punchline*
> *but refuses to follow.*

I fell in love instantly, and she, on her return, could sense my despair. She strutted around my stool like Cleopatra circling the field following a triumphant battle.

—Nice poem, I said stupidly, while she put her arms around my neck.

—You don't have to say that, lover. She kissed me in a way that she wanted me to remember.

—I . . . I met J— tonight. You know, the movie star.

—You don't have to put on airs with me, lover. We kissed again.

She lived in a walk-up just around the corner. The moon resembled a fingernail I could imagine leaving long marks.

—Hog, Mesha, Sartine, she said, by way of introduction. These must have been the names of the figures she indicated, whose impressions were as faint, at that hour and in that condition, as the outlines of hunters on the walls of ancient caves. They were playing some game with dice, I think, seated on the floor in the living room, listening to Stan Getz and passing around a bong.

She took me by the hand and escorted me into the next room to her bed, a mattress on the floor. Incense anointed the tapestried walls. A year later, five years, ten years later, back home, the movie stars and the hotel freak would become the fodder of many graceless stories. But Savannah—that was the gypsy's name, as I learned the next morning at breakfast—became a part of who I am, of my cool and my confidence. Sometimes that's all you take away from a wrecked chapter like that in life. Sometimes that's all that matters.

Shih Tzu

Our dog is plotting his escape. The rest of them, the kids and the wife, don't see what I see: a dog with a goal after so many years of indifference. Karen disagrees because it's my observation. The kids are older now and in tennis lessons, band, heat, and oblivious to anything but their own raw impulses. I alone bear the burden of vigilance. Some mornings, early, upon tiptoeing downstairs for a Pimm's Cup or a Xanax, I have caught him awake before anyone else pacing in front of the door to the garage or closely examining the sills beneath the tall dining room windows. When he senses me, he will either lie down at once or else stand erect at the door as though he'd been serving all night there as our loyal protector. Once he pretended to chase after a phantom mouse, but I am nobody's fool. It isn't food he wants. The dog doesn't sniff, he studies, like a structural engineer inspecting for fissures. Our Shih Tzu wants out.

We have provided him with a happy environment, we really have. Christ, the youngest used to make him birthday cards with paint-by-numbers kits. "Daddy, Morris needs a new rope toy," my daughter would say, and I would make it so. His food comes in parti-colored chunks infused with a bacon-like chemical plus real chives. He receives regular visits to the groomer, a CD of assorted family favorites that plays when he is left by himself, preventative medical care that includes vitamins and even a mini-treadmill. For years we could leave him on the porch without a leash and without fear of his bolting.

Those days are gone. The wanderlust began about a month ago. Sitting outside one day reading the obituaries, I was nursing a drink called Knife Tricks from my book of exotic cocktails (Kübler Absinthe, Root Beer, Regan's Orange Bitters #6, Liquid Minded Commissary Ice), when Morris came padding up the sidewalk alone and untethered. He pawed the screen door and when I rose to let him in, he snuck a quick, last look down the street that took me back to a teenage trauma, to a night I snuck a similar look back at the scene of a wild party, one I'd been compelled to leave early under embarrassing circumstances by my devout, stone-faced mother. Inquiries revealed that no one knew Morris had been absent. We could only speculate as to the motives for his unprecedented departure. Then, a week later, he fled again, this time in plain sight while the kids and I sprayed water at each other and at nesting birds in the backyard. The gate was open, a poodle and her master walked by, and Morris darted down the alley, stopping only briefly by the other dog before shooting around the corner in the direction of the park. My son and I ran after him. A bike cop who had found Morris was crouched down petting him when we got there, a pair of handcuffs connecting his wrist to the dog's collar. Morris's antics in the interim had been reported to the police and the pound by a woman whose cat he had chased into a slow-moving convertible. We'd arrived just in time to prevent the dog's detention.

It was then that I began keeping him on a leash at all times. He is not the same Morris. Ever since that initial desertion, he will snap his head toward any door left ajar and any window letting in the sounds of summer. I can see in his eyes the same look in the eyes of my boyhood dog Buck in the days before he ran away and was tragically killed by a milk tank truck on a highway near our home.

There are other changes. Morris's enthusiasm for the gourmet food we switched him to is clearly feigned. He's a smart dog but a poor actor. He is also horny again, more than ever. Neutered, of course, as a pup, and thus not long on libido, he acts as if able to feel again what was lost, like an amputee soldier with a vestigial urge to salute. Standing on his hind legs, he will wrap his forelegs around my calf or my wife's and look up at us amorously, especially when our emotions have risen in some fashion, as when we are yelling, or slumping alone silently after the other has stormed off, or frozen in a penitent embrace. Nor are inanimate objects off limits. He has grown fond of the pedestal to the marble table in our breakfast nook. The young plum tree in the side yard has become a humping post and a source of embarrassment before our elderly neighbors. On our walks in the park, dogs big and small are the targets of feckless mounting.

We look at each other differently, too. He knows that I know he is plotting his escape and eyes me warily. No longer master, I am jailor instead. To me, he is no more just a source of start-up conversations with passersby on week-end walks, more than a diversionary, soft presence on the couch in front of *Dancing with the Stars*. He is my charge, and I have found new purpose in my duty to save him from himself and from a dangerous world.

At times I must take measures that to others must seem stern, some have even said criminal, and yet, for the dog's own good. I have filled his half-dug holes near the fence with foodstuff laced with ipecac. A short, wire garden enclosure, barbed, now blocks the space that has formed over time between the grass and the gate's hem. After discovering deep scratches in the living room windows, it fell upon me to rub the dog's nose into the panes, as I did into the carpet after potty training accidents when he was a puppy. "Is this right?" I will say, above his nose-crushed squeal. "Is this how happy dogs behave?"

What we have between us then is a chess match. His evolutionary advantage is his ability to focus on unambiguous needs. Mine is a bigger brain. I am always one step ahead. Recently, on my long commute to work, I noticed by the gas gauge that it was Thursday, and remembered that it was the previous Thursday, as well as the one before that, that Karen had found the cushions from the patio chairs somehow removed from their place in the yard and piled, in what at first blush appeared a haphazard arrangement, on the ground a few feet from the gate. Initially, we attributed it to the wind (there had been a storm the first time), and then, realizing the unlikelihood of that, to some game played by one of the kids, both of whom refused to confess. But that day on the road I recalled that Morris was left alone and outside on Thursdays while Karen visited her therapist, Dr. Pecht, and the kids attended various classes and camps: vegan cooking, Arabic, jujitsu, I think. I rushed home. When I arrived, sure enough, there it was again, a pile of cushions, only this time, in an apparent attempt to stabilize the formation, Morris had added to its base and to weak points among its layers a number of neglected items from the yard: empty ceramic pots, planks of wood from a broken chair, the barbecue's tin ash catcher. Together with the cushions, he had guided them into a multi-tiered edifice that tapered near the top, like a giant wedding cake of domestic detritus, in what could have served an ironic secondary purpose, in fact, of commemorating his anticipated union with the wild. I watched with fascination through a turned-up slat in the kitchen blinds as he assembled the remaining ingredients. To set the final element in place, a Frisbee that had sat in the yard for more than a year and was the last portable object available, he climbed unsteadily with it to the summit, only to find, and express in a pathetic whimper, what he must have suspected all along, that he would still be unable to breach our tall white plastic fence, which might as well have been made out of concrete. He gave it a try anyway, first setting the Frisbee on top with such care that a bystander might have thought its accurate placement meant the difference between deliverance and ruin. And then . . . with a desperate leap! But alas, he fell pathetically short, slapping against the fence and scattering the parts of his assemblage before hurting his leg in a foreseeable collapse into a bed of impatiens.

After that I was compelled to restrict the dog to his kennel for more time than I care to disclose. It pained me to do it, but how else will he learn? One night I had been to The Tar Man for a couple of Smokin' Chokes (Applewood Smoked Four Roses, Cynar, maple syrup, lemon and orange zest) and to contemplate Morris's next gambit in the company of Maya behind the bar. Afterward Karen and I had a more turbulent quarrel than usual. She threw an object at me, a thick, heavy candle, as it turned out, which, from its unfamiliar position on the credenza, I later deduced she had set out beforehand with just that purpose in mind. Her aim was terrible. It missed me wildly and instead broke a window near the dining room floor. The dog, who had witnessed the whole thing, immediately tried to seize the opportunity by sprinting toward the hole despite its intimidating shards. I was only able to stop him because in reacting to avoid the projectile I had whirled in his direction and stumbled, by the grace of God, directly into his path. He had to go without food for a while after that one, I'm afraid. I thought of the move later, with Karen, and tried to somehow duplicate it as part of our rambunctious making-up intercourse, but failed.

Things have died down considerably since then. The jerky manner in which Morris shifts his head from side to side as he walks, however, which he never did before, suggests to me that he is both alert to the possibilities of flight and concerned about the repercussions of failure. I now keep a log book to help me anticipate his next stratagem, tracking not only his attempted escapes but any of his behaviors that strike me as unusual. Shih Tzu, I have learned, is Chinese for lion dog. As part of my efforts to stay one step ahead, I have begun to research his pedigree. The Shih Tzu is a cross between the Lhasa Apso, originally bred in the great monasteries of Tibet, and the royal Pekingese, a favorite for centuries of Chinese emperors in the Forbidden City. *Majestic* and *solitary* are two of the many highlighted descriptive terms in my log. I am also reading a book about China, another diversion from the joint venture contracts and oil and gas leases that otherwise dominate my waking life. My wife says I'm a reader. "You're a reader," she says, in one of her pleasanter moods. And the kids say, dryly: "Dad's a big reader."

Have I mentioned that I need help? One night I set aside the log and began reading my big glossy book about China at the kitchen table with a glass of Malbec and a bowl of Neapolitan ice cream. The kids were in the living room laughing and playing with the dog when I turned to a page with a large picture of a three-sail junk afloat in an exotic

Asian harbor. It made me think of the army for some reason, which is strange because I wasn't in very long and had little memory of it. Maybe the reason is that a poster of clipper ships was on the wall of the brig I was in for a couple weeks, about six months out of basic training. The mind is funny. I had gone AWOL for a night to attend a party in La Jolla with a young lady I'd met on leave, a contortionist with a cabaret passing through town called Teatro ZinZanni. The blemish on my record was like a small scar from a noble battle won. Her name was Zelda, like the writer's wife. Of that night I remember every organic detail.

In any event, after that the cranberry necklace Maya was wearing the last time I saw her crossed my mind, how it complemented her gray dress and green eyes, and I smiled as I got up to close the back door to keep out the chill air before setting down my wine. The kids were still laughing, which gives me a lot of joy. The dog, on the other hand, had backed off and was staring at me from a crouched position against the wall, his tail no longer wagging. When I sat down and stared back at him the same way, I crossed my arms and stopped smiling, serious about my responsibility as sentry and attentive to any detail that might help me anticipate his next maneuver. I have done my research. Inhibited by monks and eunuchs in his past, the lion dog by midlife becomes obsessed with urges he can only injure himself attempting to satisfy. My diligence, I'm afraid, may be all that stands between him and his doom. And vice versa.

Psychiatrist

She wakes up but before her eyes are open her body knows that she is alone. The odor of fried pig fat confirms that Rob is up before her, making breakfast. It's an awful stench. With her eyes still closed she runs through the mental exercises she uses to banish negative thoughts. Gradually, her brow unfurls, and she can open her eyes and embrace the morning. *It's only bacon.* The sunlight, so beautiful, slants in through the open blinds. Her smile reflects warmth as she recalls—and how could she forget?—that she is *Mrs.* Allie Martin. She vows to greet her husband of three months with the energy and optimism he deserves.

"Perfect timing," he says as they kiss. "I was just coming to wake you." He slides two poached eggs onto a plate alongside the bacon and toast he's prepared and gives her shoulder a squeeze. She grimaces, because he's disturbed a tender area he bruised the night before while they were making love; too briskly, she thought at the time, but didn't want to ruin the moment, and likewise now doesn't let him see her wince.

"Aren't you eating?"

"Mm," he takes a quick bite of toast. "I'm meeting Ben. I'm late already."

The scattered papers on the table indicate he's been working since early morning. He gathers them along with the book he takes everywhere, *Success in 10 Simple Rules.*

Ben is Ben Carlson, founder of Ben Carlson Studios, their *ben*efactor, as Rob likes to joke. Of the two BCS ballroom dance clubs in town, Ben operates the original and franchises the other to Rob, who, like the dozen other franchisees around the country, pays Ben a percentage for use of the BCS teaching system and name. Lately Rob has been trying to work out an arrangement with Ben that will grant him independence while allowing him to continue participating in the BCS showcases convened biannually, where members and instructors from all the clubs gather to perform routines on a grand stage. It's a big selling point. The show is followed by a formal ball. Allie is currently at work on two numbers, including a cha-cha with her newest Bronze student for a performance next Sunday at the first event hosted locally in years.

"How's that going?" she asks.

He kisses the top of her head. "Don't you worry," he says. "You haven't touched your breakfast."

She punctures one of the egg yolks with a fork. "Hon. Sweetie, you know I'm not eating bacon or eggs on this new diet. I'll have some melon when you're gone."

"Don't be silly, you'll need all your strength today. What time is Joe?"

She knows he knows when her lesson with Joe Stevens is, it's been marked in red on his office calendar for a week. They're trying him for the full Bronze program today, fourteen thousand dollars. "Two o'clock," she says, nibbling a piece of toast.

"Nobody needs the Bronze like Joe does. Overweight, balding, insecure."

"He understands that."

"He has to *feel* it," Rob says, squeezing her shoulders again. This is a refrain she's heard a thousand times since she began teaching there after a year as his student. She winces again, assures him that Joe feels the magic, and scoops a whole egg into her mouth as if to confirm it.

"That's my girl," he says. "I know he does."

After he leaves, Allie, having breached her diet, sees no reason not to finish her plate; then she unwraps the rest of the bacon and fries it along with four more eggs. As it all sizzles, she reviews the benefits to Joe Stevens of a two-year membership—longer individual sessions, group lessons every week, unlimited parties—before catching herself, remembering that these are not benefits but features. She begins again, this time out loud: Gracefulness. Confidence in social settings. Improved self-esteem. She must present these to Joe in a way that makes him feel like she felt when she was a student. Of course, she learned from the very best. "Dancing should be like great sex!" Rob rhapsodized during their first tango lesson. Today, with Joe, she is determined to channel that same irresistible energy.

She butters two slices of toast, eats them along with the bacon and eggs, and follows it all with yogurt and a bowl of ice cream. Joe understands. Correction: Joe feels it. He has a good teacher, she reminds herself, remembering Rule 8: Compliment yourself daily. Then she smiles to herself too, because, as Rob says, it's impossible to be negative when you're smiling, a variation of Rule 5.

Upstairs, she hangs up clothes Rob has left on the floor. Kelly wishes she were in my shoes, Allie tells herself. She would never admit it, but I know it's true, everybody says so. Even now she clings to some impossible fantasy, even though she's with Sean. I can tell when Rob works with her.

What's more, Sean isn't going to marry her. I don't know why she can't see that.

A book of matches falls from Rob's pants. He's been on the patch for weeks but still sneaks an occasional cigarette; she can tell from the odor in his hair. She hopes it isn't more than a few, because he really wants to quit, believing it hurts the studio's image. She notices they are from Mama Stuffiti's. Good. They're old. They haven't been to Mama's in five months, since the night they agreed to marry. Rob must have kept them for sentimental reasons, the dear. Only a few matches are missing. Good again, he's not sneaking too many.

She folds his pants on the way to the bathroom, where she bends over the toilet and, for the first time since her miscarriage three weeks before the wedding, sticks a finger down her throat to make herself vomit. At the sink, she wipes her mouth with the back of her hand, brushes her teeth and flosses. As she takes a dozen vitamins three at a time, she thinks, I hope Rob doesn't break with Ben the way Ben broke with Arthur Murray. What a nasty lawsuit everyone says that was! Worrying that he'd better be careful, that Ben Carlson can be vicious when money is at stake, she removes the matches again from Rob's pocket and fingers them unconsciously, before dropping them in the wastebasket and swallowing the acid residue at the back of her throat.

* * *

Ben is still at the studio when she arrives, talking to Rob at the reception desk. He greets her with a hug and holds her away at arm's length.

"Look at you," he says. "That blonde hair. Still the prettiest girl in the business. Rob, how did you corral the prettiest girl in the business?"

"She's trying Joe Stevens for Bronze today."

Allie can see her reflection distorted in Ben's large, nearly round tinted glasses. "Well, I'm sure she'll do just fine," he says, and she can make out that his eyes enlarge as he squeezes her hands. "How could he resist?" he adds, revealing that devilish smile he's perfected after thirty years of financial triumphs.

He and Rob finish talking privately while Allie changes into her dance shoes. She has a lesson with the Watsons before Joe is due in. A sweet couple, Allie's first full Bronze sale more than a year ago. Loretta was hooked from the beginning, since her introduction at their first party to some of the more advanced couples and club ambassadors. Bill Watson, hopelessly ungraceful, was less inspired but will do anything for his wife. They have time and money in their retirement and bought the whole package without the hard sell from Rob. He was so proud of her that day, the day she first knew she was in love.

When they arrive, Allie hugs them and leads them onto the floor. By now she can sleepwalk through their lessons, and her mind wanders to the other instructors. Travis is chatting with one of his lonely old ladies. Their sessions consist of him dragging them around the room as he complains about former boyfriends and they recite their list of ailments. Kelly is there also; Allie knows it first by the laugh. She contends that Kelly's chirpy laughter is phony, but Rob disagrees. He is on the floor too, with Mrs. Shapiro, running through the quickstep he's choreographed for their upcoming performance. His lessons are all smiles and grace and pinpoint instruction. The king, Allie thinks. And I . . . am the queen!

When the Watsons' lesson ends, she chats briefly with John Freeman, who is waiting for the new girl, Candy, to arrive. Then she goes over the Bronze program she's spent much of the week meticulously preparing. She retraces some of her handwriting, which could pass for type. Each of the dances Joe will learn—tango, waltz, the other standards, along with a more ambitious paso doble and a romantic bolero she's added just for him—is described in glamorous terms and dressed up in the margins with smiling faces and dancer decals. At the bottom of the last page, she's inscribed "LET'S DO IT!!!" in bulging bold letters.

Candy rushes in, late again, and escorts John onto the floor by the arm. He doesn't seem to mind that she's late, but this was a big mistake on Candy's part because they are trying John for Medley today. Rob has yet to reprimand her for her repeated tardiness, so Allie makes a mental note to speak to him about it. Joe must be running late too, which is not unusual. He doesn't answer when she calls, but he may just be stuck in traffic. In the meantime, so as not to look too anxious, she decides to work alone in the practice room on the showcase she'll be doing with her most challenging student, Reggie Morris.

As she runs through the first part of the routine, she peeks at Candy and tries to evaluate her with the eye of an owner's wife. Candy's been there less than a month, she teaches only beginners and doesn't dance with much confidence yet herself. Each day she takes a lesson from Rob. Still, she has a fluid way about her that shows potential. Her student is obviously infatuated; he doesn't care about the dancing. He's shy, you can see that, but he can't keep his eyes off her. Candy *is* attractive, with long brunette hair, full lips, and a well-proportioned figure, even if it does show signs of future plumpness. Of course beauty only goes so far in this business. You might sell a beginner's program or even a Medley package on romance, but nobody's going to spend ten or fifteen thousand dollars on Bronze just to dance with you, no matter how good-looking you are. You have to sell the feeling. Rob was so right about that. And now here he is, leaving Mrs. Shapiro alone to practice her steps. He goes over to help Candy because he thinks just like I do. They demonstrate the fox trot together. Smart. John watches and smiles. He can't do it that smoothly, of course he can't. Rob puts him at ease with a joke and some encouraging remarks (God, he's good) and then returns to Mrs. Shapiro, leaving Candy beaming and feeling more graceful than she is and more confident with her student, who longs to dance with her like Rob did. Candy will never inspire people like that, but then who can? Rob is the master.

"Where is he?" Rob says, popping his head into the practice room.

"I called but there was no answer. I left—" but Rob lets the door shut without waiting for her to finish, "a message," she says, to herself.

She knows Rob is disappointed, but what can she do? Practice her routine, that's what. Always be making yourself better. Rule 7. Joe will be there, he's only fifteen minutes late. So, she turns on the music and practices like the winner she is.

Halfway into the first run-through, she forgets the turn and backs into a crossover at the wrong moment. She repeats the whole sequence. During the split, she catches sight of Andrew practicing the tango he's prepared for Mrs. Kurtz, which is too difficult for them both. Kristina teaches a small group of Silver members. Patti, all cleavage, changes into her dance shoes, while Sean mans the music booth and pretends not to notice. Allie spins as though Reggie is there and has led her into a turn. When she stops abruptly, as the routine demands, she's facing in the direction of Candy and John again, who are holding each other in dance position, just standing there giggling. *That cunt.* What time is it?

She does the whole routine again and messes up again, distracted about Joe. Even if he doesn't show up, he'll be at the club party on Friday. All they need to do is get him in the room. He feels the magic, she knows this, and Rob is such a good closer. Everything will be okay.

She runs through the routine once more and botches it the same way.

You can bet this student of Candy's will be at the party, to see Candy again. And I'm sure Candy will be at the staff party afterward, at our house. I wish Rob hadn't done that, I'm not ready to play hostess yet. When it was just his house when we were dating, before all the mess that followed, he hosted that party and we ended up playing Suck-and-Blow all night, passing the playing cards mouth-to-mouth. How filthy! This time I'll make a dance tape, just swing and Latin. He sits next to busty Annabelle (thank God she's gone!) and sucks and blows with her all night, retrieving fallen cards from her dress, and thinks it's okay because I'm between that pimply short-timer—what was his name?—and Andrew! Christ. This time no games.

Over and over, she dances the sequence she's bungled until she has it down pat, and she commits to come in Saturday to practice the whole number until it's flawless. Joe's a half hour late. *He'd better be in an accident, that hairless pig.* He's not coming, she knows this. They'll have to try him Friday night. He's more likely to buy at a party, anyway.

He'll be in a great mood! She decides to call him one more time. In the music booth, her cell phone is at her ear when Rob pokes his head in.

"Don't bother. He called and cancelled."

She lowers the phone and feels like she should apologize. Before she can say anything, Candy approaches with her student by her side.

"Rob, do you have a minute?" she says. "John would like to talk to you about the benefits of signing up on our Medley program."

"Oh, terrific. John, is it? Let's see." He scans the room as though genuinely considering where to take them, and finally points to his right, to the only room ever used for closing. He says cheerfully, "No one's in here," before leading them in. Allie can hear them laughing through the door and thinks: I will have my turn Friday.

* * *

After the party they pull up to their house having not spoken for miles. In the garage, Allie says his name just as he slams the door, so he must not have heard her, because he goes inside without responding, leaving her alone in the car. Inside, she wipes the kitchen island and silently empties snack bags into large bowls. "You know, I've been thinking," she says finally, after clearing her throat. "Joe might not have the money after all. He might have been telling the truth."

Rob removes from the tabletop a thick cubic vase that Allie bought at an estate sale on a recent spree. He was upset when she brought it home, along with a vintage breakfast platter and another much larger amphora-shaped vase that she's been filling with corks as they go through bottles of wine. "It's possible," Rob says wryly, setting the vase on the counter at arm's length, like he's returning someone else's hysterical baby. "I suppose."

Anticipating his needs, she uncorks a bottle of Chardonnay. The alcohol-free club party had a low turnout, and that, along with Joe Stevens' refusal to purchase any portion of the Bronze program, has put him in a sour mood.

"He has two more lessons. We can try him again—"

"No," Rob interrupts. "We lost him. Anyway, that new kid, what's his name? The one who signed onto Medley this week."

She accidentally brushes an empty glass with her elbow but catches it before it hits the floor.

"Nice grab. He seemed to be having a good time."

"His name is John."

Allie helped Candy a lot by dancing with John at the party, demonstrating heel-toe, which he hadn't been taught yet, getting him to bend his knees, putting his mind on the dancing instead of on Candy.

Several cubes fall to the floor when she tries to crack ice into a bucket. Instead of picking them up, she backs onto a stool, rubs her hands through her hair, and feels like crying. Rob pours them both a glass of wine and sits beside her.

He rubs her neck. "Do you remember Rule 4?" he asks, after a long silence.

She doesn't know immediately what he's referring to. She's read much of the book, or at least leafed through it, and Rob has repeated rules to her from time to time, but sometimes he amends the rules to match his own notions of success or to satisfy his emotional prejudices. She can't always keep track, and now she looks at him searchingly. As always, an answer appears poised just beyond the luster of his hazel eyes.

"You remember," he urges.

"Put—" she offers, hesitantly.

"—the past behind you," he finishes. "Yes. Yes! Live in the now! Doesn't that make sense?"

She nods.

"We put our failures behind us and move forward." He kisses the top her head. "I'm going to get changed, they'll be here soon."

She follows him into the living room. "You don't think I could have done anything different? With Joe, I mean."

"Honey," he says, turning on the radio. "Inside, Joe knows he lost something tonight. It's his loss. We learn from it and we put our failures behind us. Right?"

"Right," she says, forcing a smile.

"Now let's put on our party mood," he says, adding on his way up the stairs, "Someday we're going to be just as big as Ben."

While he's upstairs she drinks her wine and moves the couch to create space for dancing. He's right, of course: history is *his* story, one of Rob's favorite sayings. Before he comes down, she eats half a bowl of potato chips to make up for the cold cuts and crudités she missed while they were in the office trying to close Joe Stevens. She's starting to feel better.

Patti arrives first, followed by Rick Caputo. Soon the entire staff of twelve is there, and Allie's mood turns upbeat after she puts on her favorite playlist. Greg protests at first that he dances for a living and doesn't want any part of it when he's off work, but he's pooh-poohed by the others, and within a drink or two is dancing as uninhibitedly as they are.

"I wonder if a porn star has sex when he's not performing," Travis submits during a break in the music. Before Allie can find the song she wants, Rob, on his third glass of wine, gets everyone's attention. "Listen up, everybody . . . let me take this opportunity to announce our big sales this week. Candy, as many of you know, signed up her first Medley student the other night."

Exaggerated applause elicits an obliging curtsy. "John . . . Freeman, is it? . . . is now a member. Candy is doing a wonderful job of showing him the benefits we provide." He raises his glass.

"He sees the benefits all right," Greg whispers to Sean, but loud enough that Allie can hear. *The lecher.*

She uncorks another bottle of wine. For one jaundiced moment the words *Candy* and *whore* unscramble in her head, only to scramble again instantly and vanish.

"And Rick sold another double showcase to the Forsythes," Rob continues. Rick, a veteran of foreign dance wars, as he puts it, having moved to the London club after starting with Ben at the original space, came to work for Rob, the up-and-comer, on his return to America. He sells so many programs that it's taken for granted his students will continue and upgrade. He's also the best dancer at the club besides Rob, whose little speech ends in a cul-de-sac, leaving everyone quiet. The absence of what could have been raves for a sale to Joe Stevens leaves a hole in Allie's stomach. But after restarting the music, she shakes it off and pulls Rick onto the floor to get the ball rolling again, and maybe to show off in front of Candy, who looks a little too proud of herself next to Rob in the kitchen doorway.

It's a mambo. Not a dance for beginners. *Eat that, Candy.* Allie's been working on her Latins for an instructor routine she'll perform at the showcase with Rob. Rick immediately gets her spinning. When she first started working at the club, before she was with Rob, she slept with Rick. Just once. Everyone learned about it. But because he's a notorious hound, the backlash was minimal, unlike with Michel, or Brandon, whose departures following their brief affairs with her triggered an unflattering sequence of gossip.

Rick pushes her away and then reels her in before reversing her direction unexpectedly by hooking her hip with his raised lower leg. The others stop dancing and egg them on.

He was an original in bed, too, she remembers that. For a time she had dreams about it, in which in addition to sex, she found herself eating or preparing Italian desserts: ricotta cheesecake, tiramisu. She's reminded of that as they finish the mambo, with him extending her over his arm to form a conjoined human arch. Amid playfully hyperbolic whooping and hollering from the others, she looks to see if Candy is paying attention. The upside-down kitchen is empty. Rick straightens her up and bows dramatically while she remains standing.

"Where is Robby?" she asks no one in particular. The bathroom and the patio are vacant when she checks.

"Has anyone seen Rob?" she repeats on her return. The music has stopped. The others are talking and ignore her. Sean suggests they play a game.

"How about Suck-and-Blow?" Greg suggests immediately.

"No!" Allie cries. "No Suck-and-Blow."

"What's Suck-and-Blow?" Kristina asks.

"No Suck-and-Blow," Allie repeats. She opens and closes the door to the extra bedroom. "I'm trying to find Rob."

"Oh, come on, don't be a party pooper," Greg says. "Not everyone was here the last time."

"I mean it," she says, accompanied by a stern, this-is-my-house-now glare.

Kelly says, "I think I saw him go upstairs with Candy."

"Fine," says Greg, quick to adapt. "What about something else?"

"I know a good game," Patti says. "It's called Psychiatrist."

Allie isn't listening. She calls Rob's name and then hurries up the stairs. The bedroom door is closed. "Rob, our guests want to play a game," she calls out just before entering. The room is empty.

Downstairs, Patti is explaining the game to Greg. "I can't say until someone is chosen to be 'it.' That person has to figure out the rules."

When Allie returns, Greg tells her, "Allie, you're it. For nixing our Suck-and-Blow."

"Shut up, I can't find Robby," she says, with unintentional ferocity. She's a little dizzy from her second glass of wine, but in the kitchen pours another one anyway. It's there that she smells smoke.

"Honey . . ." Rob gasps when she opens the door to the garage. He backs away clumsily from his position by the workbench, several inches from Candy.

"You caught me," he says vaguely, and then holding up a cigarette adds, "Only my second one today," before putting it out in a flower pot.

"I should have stopped him," Candy says. She is also smoking.

"Yes, you should have."

Allie notices two of the fluorescent lights in the ceiling fixtures are flickering. "They want to play a game," she says after a pregnant silence.

"Great! Good, let's play a game." He squeezes between her and the car. "You can finish that inside if you want," he says to Candy from the door. "If that's all right with you, hon."

Allie doesn't speak or turn. "No, that's okay," Candy says, putting her cigarette out. "I'll live longer without it, right?" She laughs nervously as she pockets a book of matches from the workbench that Allie, alone after Candy and Rob have gone inside, noticed were from Mama Stuffiti's.

* * *

"Everyone sits in a semicircle like they are now except Allie. She stands in the middle and asks questions," Patti explains to everyone while Allie waits upstairs. "She can ask anything of anyone as long as it's about that person. But instead of answering for themselves, whoever she asks will answer for the person sitting to their left. Allie won't know this; she'll have to figure it out. So, if she asks Greg . . . I don't know—'Are you wearing a blue shirt?'—even though he is wearing a blue shirt, he will say—?"

"No," Greg says.

"Right. Because Kristina, on his left, is not wearing a blue shirt. But, if he wants to—and here's the key—he can lie and answer yes, in which case Kristina says 'Psychiatrist.' Whenever anyone says 'Psychiatrist' everyone gets up and sits somewhere else, with someone new on their left."

"I don't get it," Kristina says. "Why do I say 'Psychiatrist'?"

"That's what you say when the person answering the question answers incorrectly, as it applies to you. If they answer correctly, you don't say anything, and the game goes on—Allie asks someone else a new question. But if they answer incorrectly, you say 'Psychiatrist.' They might answer wrong on purpose or because they don't know the right answer for you, but either way, you say 'Psychiatrist.' 'Psychiatrist' is just the name. It could be called 'Eggplant' or 'Sapphire' or whatever, but it's not."

"She'll get it right away," Candy says.

47

"Well, maybe, but you try to fool her, that's the thing. Don't be obvious. Oh, and we should encourage her to ask personal questions: sexual questions, or whatever. Instead of 'What are you wearing?' something like, 'Have you ever had sex in a public place?' or 'How many partners have you had in the last five years?' It's way more fun that way."

In the bathroom upstairs, Allie is throwing up potato chips. When she finishes, she sits on the lid, confused and lightheaded. He'd been having a couple drinks after work with Ben, he told her two weeks ago Monday, on business. And there was another night, allegedly with Ben, when Rob tiptoed in while she was half asleep. Allie remembers meeting Rob's first wife when she was still in the business, an extraordinary dancer, elegant, much closer to Rob's age, and her parting words whispered tellingly at the showcase in that dazzling hotel ballroom in Denver: *Keep a close eye on him, honey.* Of course, Allie had heard the rumors. If they were true, she would change him, that's how determined she was. She had changed him. His consent to wed after a year of dating was an admission of change, having vowed never again to marry. He told her that. He assured her his willingness to marry was about more than just the baby. And when she later lost it, he was the one who insisted on going through with the wedding, already planned for the weekend of his family reunion.

She examines her pale complexion in the mirror. She had changed him. He was smoking a cigarette, that's all she saw. Everything else can be explained. When she hears her name, she splashes water on her face and joins the others, self-assured.

"Just ask anything to begin with," Patti advises. "When you get the hang of it, you can be a little bolder."

Rob has mixed a pitcher of Sangrias and is walking around the sectional pouring everyone a drink. Once he settles in, Allie begins by asking Andrew how long he's been in the business. "Thirty years" is Andrew's response, an obvious falsehood. On his left, Patti says "Psychiatrist," and everyone changes places.

"It's simple," Allie says. "You don't answer the question honestly." Patti tells her that's not it, and to continue.

Allie asks Rick who his favorite student is, knowing that he, like Rob, favors Heather Lamb. Rick answers honestly, but then Kristina, seated next to him, says "Psychiatrist," and they all move again.

Allie pours herself another drink. Sean does a spot-on impersonation unrelated to the game, of Rick rumbaing eye-to-eye with Heather Lamb—at least Allie assumes it's unrelated. When she asks the next question, nobody says "Psychiatrist." She thinks, maybe it's not *what* they answer but *the way* they answer.

She asks more questions. Rob replenishes drinks after everyone changes places for the third time. Allie thinks: Sometimes they tell the truth, other times they lie. Sometimes they get up and move, but often they don't. Once in a while someone says "Psychiatrist," but just as often they remain silent. She notices Suzanne can't stop eating snack food and wonders if it's part of the game. They change places after a lie, she notes, but not always; they move after the truth sometimes, too. Where do they move? *Damn it!* She hasn't paid any attention to that. Now she's really confused.

"Don't be such a prude, Allie," Greg says, after they'd been playing the game for half an hour. "Open it up a little."

Everyone is laughing and having a good time except her. She tries to play along, to act the good hostess despite everything. Rule 6: Don't be afraid to step out of your comfort zone. She asks Kristina when she lost her virginity, Andrew how many men he's slept with. His response—fewer than fifty—elicits a self-congratulatory chuckle from Travis, to his left, followed by "Psychiatrist" and howls of laughter as everyone changes places again. Allie's frustration intensifies with each round. Why doesn't Rob sense her alienation and come to her aid? Are they laughing at her for failing to crack the code?

Think! Allie. The person next to the one I question sometimes says "Psychiatrist." When?

To be funny, she asks Sean, who is straight, if he would consider sleeping with Matthew McConaughey. He makes a big show, stating that although Mr. McConaughey is a gorgeous, rich movie star, he, Sean, is so happy with his mate he would never consider cheating, even with him. Kelly, to his left, busts up the room when she takes the bait and says "Psychiatrist," and again they all switch places.

Allie has a revelation: they are answering for the person on their left! Rob and Candy are seated next to each other now. Everyone is still laughing, and Candy, nearly convulsive, falls halfway into Rob's lap.

Blurt it out! Allie thinks. Get the game over with! They are answering for the person on their left, and . . . when they answer wrong, the person says "Psychiatrist." That's it!

Before she can say anything, she thinks she hears someone mutter the name Joe Stevens and spins around. They *are* laughing at her. Was that Patti mocking her recent failure? *Or that jealous bitch, Kelly?* She might have imagined it. She looks to Rob's face for answers and finds it red with mirth. He bends forward to put down his drink as a hand lands on his right knee.

"Candy!" Allie says the name so loudly the room goes quiet. For a moment she isn't sure what to say or why she shouted. Then she remembers.

"Have you ever slept with the person sitting to your right?"

"Whoa," Greg says. He sits to Candy's right but understands, as everyone does, especially Allie, that Candy will be answering for Rob, to her left, and that the question is posed to determine if the two have been having an affair. The grandfather clock strikes one. A strap on Allie's blouse slips off, exposing her bony shoulder. Candy looks directly at her and, to give Rob an easy way out by remaining silent, lies. "No," she says, without flinching. Allie doesn't blink either. She rotates toward her husband with the desperate eye of an impossible, contradictory appeal: don't say anything, her mind pleads, my love, my life—but be honest! A cold glare is all he offers in return. Fine. Good. Silence is good. But just when she believes she's survived, Rob opens his big mouth.

"Psychiatrist."

Immediately, he feigns confusion: he'd misspoken, had failed to understand. But it's too late. No one moves, even though the rules of the game demand it. They all fidget or sip their drinks without making eye contact with anyone. There. *There are your facts, idiot!* They did it. Everyone knows about it. And you're a fool.

Candy sinks deep into the cushions. Greg stands up first, not to change seats—the game is clearly over—but with a consoling hand extended toward Allie, who, trembling and half-encircled, appears more isolated than ever. She stares at Rob, her hands crisscrossed over her chest, gripping her upper arms, until Greg touches her shoulder, at which point she flees the home that is no longer her asylum.

"I told you we should have played Suck-and-Blow," Greg says, but no one even smiles. Rob rises with a sigh and heads after her.

*　*　*

The parquet dance floor is surrounded by three dozen circular tables draped in white tablecloths and set for the evening's dinner. A pair of long tables topped with ribbons and trophies stand behind a microphoned podium, where the master of ceremonies is often interrupted or replaced altogether by Ben Carlson at his discretion. Above the stage, by a thin cable, hangs an ornate chandelier that aptly reflects the stylized ritual taking place below.

Allie stands at the edge of the dance floor with her student, Reggie Morris. She is the only one from her club not cheering for Andrew and Mrs. Kurtz as he leads her through steps barely recognizable as tango. Instead, she replays the events leading up to her decision a day and a half earlier to give Rob another chance. He caught her in her car outside the house and they drove to a forest preserve, where she cried and listened to his excuses. He admitted his betrayal. He pleaded for forgiveness, promising to be true and to fire Candy, whom, to be fair to everyone, he would steer to Ben Carlson for an interview. Back at the house, where the party had broken up, she kept up her resistance. But Rob was determined to make it up, and somehow they ended up in bed. The sex was dreadful, and rough, a pantomime of suppressed anger. She scratched his back, he bit her neck in retaliation, hard enough to leave a mark. Later that morning, she awoke by herself, unable to move. Her period had begun, and she was aware that her feelings toward Rob were not so much different from hatred. Now, across the room, he complements Ben, the aspirant at his mentor's side, pretending as he watches Andrew fumble through his routine to be proud and impressed, although she knows he's been considering Andrew's dismissal. Rob is taller than Ben and striking in black tie and tails, his confidence limited only by its relation to his neighbor's. Older and much richer, Ben's self-satisfaction is absolute. Without waiting for the routine to end, he directs Rob into the lobby.

Recalling Friday night's scene, Allie wonders if she will ever live down the humiliation. She has spoken no more than she must to her club mates, distracting herself by repeatedly going over her routines. Her dress, a high-slit cobalt blue number with spangles that Rob bought her with this event in mind, has generated only one compliment, and that from Joe Stevens, with whom she was very curt. No money for a showcase or a portion of the Bronze but he shows up to get the last dollar's value from his expiring limited membership. *Pig. No wonder you're alone.* Before leaving the house, she decided a proper tribute to her husband, one he deserved, was to maximize the effect of the dress by leaving her undergarments behind.

She and Reggie are set to follow Kelly, who spins onto the floor at her student's lead. Their paso doble opens dramatically. Through the open double doors across the room, she can see Ben and Rob in the lobby conferring in private. Following a brief exchange they shake hands, and ceremonial smiles slither across their faces that from a distance blur the line between them. Something has happened and Allie knows what it is. He walks even taller, Rob does, when he reenters the ballroom. Ben remains at the doorway overseeing the fruit of his life's labor. Rob stops to watch the routine, grinning uncontrollably, an embodiment of ambition realized. Before it ends, he crosses the room, unable to restrain himself, allowing her to see him smile broadly even though he knows it's too soon after their reconciliation to express joy, that it undermines his declaration of shame. Allie can sense his dilemma. In that instant she recognizes how all that has happened between them in the last two years has been like scenes in a play whose long run is coming to an end, a play in which Rob is a promising supporting actor and she is an extra with no lines. Something has happened, she knows what it is all right, and he can remove his makeup now and savor the success of his performance before preparing for his next role, the first of many starring ones.

"He's letting us go," he says softly, so that Reggie won't hear. "Ben is." She can see how difficult it is for him to play it cool, she can still admire his control, knowing how badly he wants to rejoice, to broadcast his triumph.

"He just agreed to it. With the terms we talked about."

"You're kidding," Allie says. "That's wonderful." She is certain now that she feels nothing for him but contempt.

Kelly's routine ends thunderously, a real crowd-pleaser. Reggie cannot stop fidgeting. She reaches for his hand. "We're up. It'll be okay." Even though she was unable to practice the day before like she'd planned, having been up all night with Rob, she trusts she can back-lead Reggie through the performance if he falters.

Rob leans closer as the crowd applauds. "This is what I always wanted," he says, barely able to contain his pleasure. "My independence."

When the clapping dies out, Ben Carlson is at the microphone introducing her routine.

"—from our Metro East club here in town, Reggie Morris and his instructor Allie Martin will perform a cha-cha."

The dance is simple. She choreographed it with Reggie's limitations in mind. She watches him closely, so she can help him recover from any inevitable missteps. At the same time, she remains conscious of Ben Carlson, who has receded from the podium to the entranceway, where a blonde woman in street clothes is greeting him coyly. Allie loses sight of them as she's double-spun to the edge of the dance floor. Joe Stevens looks on, his arms crossed, resting on his fat belly. Too late for you, mister. *Cheapskate. Loser.*

Rejoining her, Reggie steps immediately into fifth position. In the same moment, she tries to back-lead him into a crossover. Was that right? No, Reggie was right! A quick spin disguises her mistake, but there is Rob in front of her when she twirls, alone, independent (*the bastard*), with a disapproving glare that stops her cold, like a wrench thrust between gears.

She stumbles on the edge of the parquet and falls to one knee. It is Candy she recognizes in that instant, the one speaking to Ben by the door. She has dyed her hair blonde. They stop talking when Allie falls, reacting instinctively to the audience's gasps. Reggie freezes, helpless and terrified. She gets up quickly, finds a place in the music to pick it up again, leading him back, trying to will away her mistake along with his fear and disappointment. Then she sees Greg suppressing a laugh. Always concealed giggles from this guy. Another turn with Rob watching them anxiously. A stillness underscores the scene as Reggie, whom she also despises now (*if he could lead, this wouldn't have happened!*), raises one arm to turn her again, remembering to hold his hand stiff. She has taught him well, *the clod*, although even with his hand held properly, their arms raised as one, she manages to free herself with a slick maneuver for a final sequence of her own spontaneous design.

Rob and Greg will recognize her improvisation for what it is. Ben, Candy, Joe Stevens, and the others are not aware of her extemporizing until they notice Reggie shuffle stupidly and then stop altogether and watch dumb like the others, watch Allie spin three, four, five times, and persist in spinning even after Rob has motioned to the sound man to cut off the music. No one knows what is happening. The first words spoken, by Rob—"That's enough"—do not reach their intended target, instead rising and dissipating in the hushed ballroom like the smoke from one of his squelched-out cigarettes. Ben Carlson leaves Candy as Allie's whirling continues. She adds an unexpected twist she considers timely, even artful, a deft unzipping of her new dress, which falls limply to the floor. It spins with her, tangled in her feet as Rob rushes forward, his previous euphoria displaced by a stunned and embarrassed rage. Ben likewise hurries in her direction. He and Rob remove their tuxedo jackets as they advance, to stifle her mad, endless spinning, to cover her emaciated bare body.

This is me naked, she thinks, as they descend upon her, jackets raised, like two outraged Draculas. *Meat on a spit* is how she imagines it first. *A human corkscrew . . . a child's top . . . an egg beater . . .* as her ideas about herself begin to rapidly unwind.

Lurch

I found Lurch finally in the back room of the Lavender Club playing poker. This, after his hostess at the Black Dolphin had told me to be careful, he had a bug up his ass, and after asking about him at Tiki Taco, often his last stop before hitting the casinos.

"You owe me money," I said, just like that. I was that desperate. He had just tossed pocket threes into the pot after Morro called his bluff.

"I owe *you* money. That's funny."

"Five hundred dollars."

He pushed back his chair. "Sit down. You'll feel better."

Lurch stood six foot seven and I don't mean in high heels. If the top of his head were any flatter you could shoot marbles on it. He poured himself a beer from the lone tap.

"I got a tip in the ninth," I said, sidestepping the table. I showed him my watch. "It's half past three."

"Sit down."

Uncle Jake pushed his way out of the bathroom clutching his ribs and suckling for breath. He folded onto the couch, reeking of vomit.

"What happened to him?"

"Accident," said Boston Phil, cutting into a stack of checks. "Walked into Lurch's fist by mistake." Phil had a singular aversion to pronouns. The Boston part of his nick-name defied explanation since he was born and raised in

Minneapolis. "Phil" was also a nickname. It was short for Philadelphia.

Uncle Jake moaned a letter to his dying mother. "He's got no trust," Lurch added, giving Jake a look you could use to break into a vault.

"I'm in," Jake gasped.

"You can't even stand up." Lurch held out his beer but Jake pressed it away.

"I'm in, damn it!"

"Suit yourself."

The room had a comfortable feel, like a baby's crib or a prisoner's cell. A cylindrical boiler clanged like a submarine in rhythm with a trio of hissing periscopes. In the next room the familiar crack of billiard balls meant that money would be changing hands, only none of it was mine.

Angela came in and passed around bowls of chili. "All right," Morro said when she left, "are we going to play cards or sing campfire songs?" He had shuffled the deck so many times it was back in order.

"Look," I said to Lurch confidentially. "I got *rent*." I wasn't the only one in the room sweating. "Take a Powder's at six-to-one."

"I tell you I don't got it," he said. Uncle Jake groped his way to the table. Lurch looked at me with the same sympathy that a giant looks at a dwarf.

"I can probably get it for you," he said finally. "If."

"If what?"

"If you're steady in the stand."

"What the hell does that mean?"

I hadn't eaten lunch, and the chili he took a forkful of smelled like the breeze in God's garden. "If you're patient," he explained.

I was getting anxious. "It's three thirty."

"Yeah," he said. "I can tell time."

I drove. His idea, not a very good one, was to parlay his remaining two bills on a craps table at the Argosy, using a system taught to him by a skinny waitress there named Rae Ann. In the car I asked stupidly, "What makes you think it'll work?"

"I did the math," he said, before spitting out window. My Hyundai could barely contain his compressed frame.

I had no better options. Lurch was good for it if he won. He did know something about money management. When I worked there, before my arrest, he would often win big on my blackjack table. That's how we came to know each other and how he came to accept me into his crew, even though he detested dealers. He was the one who posted my bond and recommended his lawyer, who got me off with community service and a program that Lurch himself had completed, for degenerate gamblers.

The system, involving a dubious combination of place bets and come bets, initially failed. Sitting box was Vincent DiCarlo, a cannonball with imaginary mob affiliations. His reputation rested on having taken a baseball bat to a dealer he'd learned was screwing his wife. Lurch started in immediately.

"How's that wife of yours doing?"

"She's coming along."

"She get you that tie?"

"What, you don't like it?"

"It looks like you got it free with a full tank of gas."

Everyone there knew Lurch. People, even DiCarlo, took his shit because he provided action. He never tipped even when he won big, which only seemed to make him meaner.

One time he colored up eight thousand and one dollars on a dice game, almost all of it winnings. As he gathered up the five-hundred-dollar checks and the single white one and started to leave the table, the boxman asked loudly, tongue firmly in cheek, if he hadn't forgotten something, meaning maybe it wouldn't hurt for a change if he tossed in the extra buck as a toke. "Yeah," Lurch said, "come to think of it." Then he pointed in turn at the smirking boxman, stickman, and two base dealers and said "Fuck you, fuck you, fuck you, and fuck you" before walking out the door. In another legendary episode, he tore up his last Benjamin and sprinkled it into a moving roulette wheel to prove how little he cared about the winnings he'd lost back after being ahead almost four thousand dollars.

This time he won. I gave Rae Ann a big kiss and she slapped me. When Lurch handed me the five bills, I was off to the Woodlands, where I arrived in time to purchase a chili cheese dog and bet Take a Powder to win, place, and show, just minutes before he faded in the stretch and finished out of the money.

That left me with eighty-five dollars. I went back to the casino and sat down at a blackjack table next to the woman I'd run the scam with that had gotten me fired—just some pretty Vietnamese who owned a nail shop and used to play on my game and give me a hard-on. I would tip her off to my hole card depending on the finger I used to point at her hand. My thinking was that helping her would get me laid, but that did not happen. Soon every Vietnamese in the place was showing up at my table expecting the same advantage. Just nickel-and-dime stuff or we would have all gone to prison for conspiracy.

"How's it going?"

"Go away," she said. "You bad guy."

She got that right. I always found it strange they let me back in there after what happened. I assumed it was because I usually lost. When I worked there and caught somebody cheating or counting cards, the supervisors invariably told me not to do anything about it. They would call upstairs to make sure the guy was on camera, and if he lost, they would let it go at that. If he won, they would stop him at the cage before he cashed out and take him into the back room for a little *chat*.

I asked DiCarlo if he'd seen Lurch, because now I needed to borrow money.

"They took him out."

"What does that mean?"

"Security. They put him in a cab."

"Any particular reason?"

He was filling out a comp for Binnie the Big. When Binnie walked away, he said, "He pissed on a dealer."

"*What?*"

"Which word didn't you understand?"

Even though I needed the loan I was glad Lurch was gone. Back in the day, he was the one who got everyone there calling me Horshack after that goofy character I look like from *Welcome Back, Kotter*. I got the details from Linh, the Vietnamese woman I mentioned. I guess Lurch got a little drunk and started to lose, and yeah, he pissed on a dealer. Pulled out his junk beneath a pai gow table and urinated on the poor old guy's shoes.

"You bad guy," Linh repeated, but I could see that she didn't mean it. She was doing pretty well at baccarat and had an empty seat next to her. "Sit down," she said, moving her purse. The night had a happy ending. We had some fun, I won a few bucks, and she loaned me the rest of the rent money.

When Lurch first started gambling, he would come in with a satchel full of hundred-dollar bills and make call bets on a dice game while the boxman counted them out, sometimes losing ten grand before the tally was complete but still cracking wise. Everyone loved Lurch back then, when his name was Ted, before he and I became pathetic. One night after things started to turn and he was alone on my game, out of nowhere he muttered, "My father used to beat the crap out of me whenever I complained about the cold on a hunting trip." Everybody's got reasons for everything, I suppose. Until then he'd been sitting there silently while I shuffled.

Later, much later, months after the night I'm describing, Lurch went to prison for arson, so deep had he gone into hock that he burned down his own restaurant for the insurance money. The night of the fire a first responder found him lying headlong down a slope with his palms in the air, like he was holding up the heavens or defending himself against the flames. It may not seem like it, but Lurch had more than a whisper of greatness in him. That genius might have flourished had his thirst for adrenalin not turned every last day into Saturday night.

Scripts

Marty and I were seated at the bar next to a regular we called Johnny Vegas, who was trying to convince me again to write his life story. The owner had told him I was a writer. Johnny had dealt dice on the wrecking crew at the Stardust in Las Vegas during the late 1970s. He'd worked the high-limit games for the whales and celebrities and had encounters with many of the real-life people the characters in the movie *Casino* were modeled after. Johnny envisioned his own story as a screenplay. In his mind, the young hotshot Johnny would be played best by Leonardo DiCaprio.

The more he drank, the more menacing Johnny became. His depictions of meeting Elvis and having an affair with the Sharon Stone character from the movie were colorful enough, but the only emotion that rang true was the bitterness he expressed when he was intoxicated and let details slip about his relationship with his own father. Pete Disparti had been a bag man for the mob when Johnny was growing up. Johnny's belligerence when he drank came across as an unconscious effort to transform himself into the wise guy he never was, it seemed to me only to impress the ghost of his family's impenetrable patriarch. For a time, I tried to shoehorn Johnny's rage into an idea I'd been kicking around about the way themes repeat themselves in our lives and across generations. In the end, the fit felt strained. That night he was slurring his words, alternately muttering threats under his breath in the direction of a man at the end of the bar who was whispering affections to his amused female companion. Prompted, perhaps, by the couple's flirting, or else by the badly concealed dysfunction that characterized Johnny's biography, Marty persuaded me to move to a table, where after another round of drinks he confided a personal history of his own.

* * *

Marty is a new friend, a lawyer I met less than a year ago, not long after he married his current wife Anna, a colleague of my wife Susan's. As a young man he had wanted, like everyone else he knew in his hometown of Los Angeles, to be a screenwriter, so much so that he moved with a friend of his after college to New Orleans, where they planned to write and set the movie they believed would win them both an Oscar. Needless to say, they were kidding themselves. The friend had asthma and an alcohol problem and left town on the advice of a doctor after two months, at which point they had completed only fifty pages of a third-rate neo-noir. Marty did a lot of drinking himself after that, alone in their unfurnished loft on Canal Street. One day he was sitting on the stoop, twirling the cherry in a Monte Carlo and considering his next move, when he noticed a young woman walking in his direction. She wore a low-cut, mini print dress, cat-eye sunglasses, and heels, and had the kind of figure, as Marty put it, in his faux–Philip Marlowe accent, "that made you want to have sex with her."

He meant to stop her, to say something smart as she passed, but a man alone in a strange city with no money or prospects lacks confidence. Maybe that's what he should have said. She kept her eyes on him, he claimed, during her long, patient approach, and slowed down as she neared. In front of him she stopped, and saved him the embarrassment of a stunned silence by removing her sunglasses and saying, in a voice as mysterious and alluring as Faye Dunaway or Jane Greer, "I am so lost."

"Who isn't?" Marty quipped, and that loosened him up. They flirted. Soon she asked him to have a drink at a place called Molly's. The whole thing felt like a movie. On the way to the bar, the owner of a voodoo shop he knew stopped him to say hello. A block later, a restaurant manager he'd played cards with yelled "Hey, Marty!" from a sidewalk café and tossed him an apple. He couldn't have choreographed a better scene to impress a potential flame if he was Bob Fosse.

She was in town for a few days from New York where she sang lead in an all-girl band called Boomerang Departure. Her name was Kate Richmond. They hit it off immediately. At Molly's, he told her a story about his stepmother's recurrent stints in the theater. She explained how the treble clef tattoo on her ankle reminded her forever of her only sanctuary as a child. They might have talked all day and into the night, as he imagined it: made love, gone to breakfast, rented a movie, planned a wedding, bore children, fought over money and relative sacrifice, succeeded—although not as much as they had hoped—and died in the same house within months of each other at approximately their average life expectancy at birth. Except that, during the second hour, she casually unraveled their fates.

"We have to be back in New York the day after tomorrow," she said. "Where should we go in the meantime?"

"*We?*"

"Me and my boyfriend. He could only get off work until Monday."

Marty chuckled. He did not answer. He asked the bartender for another beer—just one, for himself, even though hers was empty and he had an almost full one in front of him. This was the first he'd heard of any boyfriend.

With me, Marty bristled, as if the incident were much more recent than it was. He ordered another scotch. "I thought about telling her she should go to hell, that's where. She and her boyfriend, whoever he was. Leading me on. Parading around in that dress. In that *dress*. Jesus."

He was cool to her when they parted. The next day, however, as he was walking to lunch in the Quarter, she happened to pass by him in a rented convertible driven by the boyfriend.

"This is Randy," she said, when she had him pull over. Randy nodded without turning down the car radio, which was playing loud enough that they had to raise their voices to be heard.

"This boyfriend Randy had dark, wavy hair," Marty said to me, "as dark as mine. He looked to be about five eleven, maybe a buck eighty, mid-twenties. Angular, Roman features. His nose and the line of his jaw were cut sharp. He had big ears." Marty gestured at his own disproportionate ears. "Any of this sound familiar? Deep-set brown eyes," he continued, opening his eyes wide, "hooded, like awnings." Here he squinted at me and waited.

"What?" I said, because it seemed like he was expecting me to comment.

"Me. Her boyfriend looked like me. Uncanny. More like me than any man I have ever seen, before or since."

Kate and her boyfriend who looked like Marty flew back to New York the next day, and that could have been the end of it. But here's the curious part: Marty and Kate would meet again, roughly twenty years later.

It happened like this: Marty returned to Los Angeles following that errant summer in the South. He kicked around for a bit taking jobs as a skip tracer, a process server, a mystery shopper, before deciding on law school, where he met his first wife, Alice. They have two daughters, now close to maturity. Marty worked at a large firm right out of school before taking over his father's criminal defense practice when his father retired.

When the kids were in their early teens, he and Alice divorced. There was no other woman by that point, or man, for that matter; they were simply unhappy together. At first, it was a relief to be on his own again. But it wasn't long before he grew lonely.

About then, his youngest daughter persuaded him to sign up for Facebook. She recognized his loneliness and argued that Facebook and e-dating and other social media could help where his initial efforts to reestablish a social life had failed. Reluctant at first, but burdened by guilt and wanting to maintain a close relationship with his children, Marty relented. As it turned out, he was glad he did. He reconnected with one or two old friends and killed a bunch of hours in neutral that might otherwise have been spent in emotional reverse in bars or with late-night TV.

One evening he looked up Kate Richmond. He remembered her name after all those years, he said, because . . . well, because she had the kind of figure that made you want to have sex with her. Also, that her old boyfriend looked so much like Marty had stuck in his head.

Now here's the part that makes the story real—or unreal, depending on how you look at it. She had recently moved to Los Angeles and was living less than an hour from his home in Redondo Beach. Man can transplant livers and map the genetic code, but no one yet has devised a formula for coincidence, luck, or infatuation. He got in touch. And, to his amazement, she remembered him, too. She had been on her own for ages. Four years after they'd first met in New Orleans, she married her longtime boyfriend Randy, Marty's doppelgänger, but divorced him eleven months later. There had been other men since then, of course, but no marriages or children. She had moved to California, finally, for a last stab at reviving her dormant singing career. On the day she and Marty met for lunch, they got together later for dinner, too. They slept together that night and went to breakfast and a matinee the following afternoon. In three months, they were married.

And so it was that they were able to emerge from a labyrinth of midlife desperation by following a trail of bread-crumbs let fall in their youth. Though their circumstances remained otherwise unchanged, the disappointments and routine that had previously plagued their days seemed to endure, at least for a time, only in memory.

The euphoria was short-lived. Kate missed New York like a salmon misses fresh water. They drank a lot, and they fought. Worse, she wanted a child before it was too late. "Surprise!" he said. "It's already too late." He'd had a vasectomy. They should have talked earlier. Besides, he countered, when she reminded him that they were reversible, the burdens of his existing paternal obligations still consumed him. His eldest daughter, he cited by way of example, was just then considering leaving school and moving in with a much older man who was still bouncing from one bad job to another—"A musician, not surprisingly!"—and Marty considered it his duty, after consulting the oracle of his own past, to dissuade her.

No. No more kids, he insisted. Much too old. "And so are you," he determined with finality.

One of Kate's last comments to him before filing for divorce and returning to New York was, "You're just like Randy, only worse. Go fuck yourself."

Tennessee

Traffic came to a stop. The woman behind him hit her brakes and leaned on her horn, mouthing invective. The smog hovering above the canyon cast her face in a sepia shroud, and together with the wordless, exaggerated movement of her lips reminded him of silent movies. In a final fit of vulgarity, she knifed her head out the window and crudely cut her way into the age of sound. Wash gave her the finger in the rearview mirror before turning sharply onto a ramp toward the belly of Los Angeles.

Soon he was lost. Two lefts and a right landed him on La Cienega but going away from the university. A bus that pulled out without signaling caused him to swerve and spill his coffee. When it inched through a turn belching black exhaust, he had to accelerate to make it through the intersection. Cussing, he caught a glimpse of a young man on the bus wearing an old-fashioned hat, a fedora. In profile he had an old-fashioned face, too, lined with struggle, that in that instant appeared recognizable. Although he couldn't say for sure if he knew the man, it nagged at him for the next block or two. Without understanding why, he felt sure that the man's identity held some deep, personal significance for him, and that determining its meaning would somehow result in a feeling of shed burdens, like the slow distancing of a ship from jetsam discarded at sea. He checked his watch; he was running late. After weighing the inconvenience to his students against the lure of some unfathomable relief, he decided to loop around to see if he could find the bus again before class.

He wound up on a residential street on his way back to the main artery. A new hit song by The Pretenders, "Talk of the Town," played on the radio station he'd had on all week, part of an effort to better relate to his students and to his daughter, who was also a student, but hours away in the Theater and Performance Studies department at Berkeley. He hadn't seen this neighborhood in years. Low leafless trees seemed leafless for no discernible reason. Above them, and above the orange and yellow stucco homes loomed tall, sparse palm trees leaning ominously inward. His eyes followed them up to a dome of clouds arranged in fluffy, sea-like ripples. He could have been imagining the hatted man, just as that very morning his wife assured him he'd been imagining another man, dressed all in black, seen bounding into the hills above their terraced garden.

Sam Washevsky was in his tenth year of teaching Advanced Editing Techniques following a middling career directing Hollywood movies. As a young man, he had signed up for the war and been injured at the Battle of Hürtgen Forest. He'd enlisted despite having to abandon a promising start in the film business, and despite having been briefly, and later regrettably, a member of the Communist Party. In a cliché that could have been central to one of his later films, he married the nurse who had supervised his convalescence. Wash's career picked up where it left off on his return from Europe. Hollywood in those days was a town where the men you laughed with on Tuesday at Musso & Frank's might deny by week's end that you were ever acquainted.

He recognized a Fotomat and found his way to Olympic. The buses he pulled alongside were filled with faraway strangers. Those who noticed him seemed to react with disapproval. One cocked his head sideways and sneered, another man's eyebrows scrunched inward accusingly, a woman holding a terrier pulled the dog close to stifle its growl. The clouds and the smog melded. Pedestrians thrust open palms his way at crosswalks.

The Fotomat reminded him of a scene on the steps of an old courthouse. He and his current wife, along with their infant daughter and his son, a child of seven at the time, were approached by angry picketers and scurried away, with Rebecca pulling the boy's head to her hip and covering his free ear with her hand. Another image, years later: his son, by then a young man, visiting Wash's home from school, encountered at breakfast reading a book about the Golden Age of Cinema, then closing it abruptly and leaving the room in response to his father's "Good morning."

When he located the bus he'd seen earlier, he followed it into Koreatown, maneuvering until he'd satisfied himself that none of its passengers wore hats or looked even remotely familiar. The man might have gotten off, he supposed. But driving away he turned back and saw that the wrinkled face on the side panel was a familiar old washed-out actor in an advertisement for Fedor's coffee. The mind plays tricks.

You might experience some occasional forgetfulness, the doctor had warned in his heavy French accent, unwrapping the bandages around Wash's head. Mood swings was another likely effect, as were visions and nightmares, repeated to him by his nurse, Madeline, in the days before they'd started dating. Wash experienced none of those symptoms. Except for an occasional angry outburst, he had made a complete recovery. He and Madeline married and settled into a quiet bungalow in Pasadena, where he was able to resume his career in pictures almost immediately.

So that wasn't it. He *had* seen someone, young but old-fashioned and recognizable, who might have bent over when Wash neared, or backed behind his seat-mate, or removed his hat and put on some kind of disguise. What Wash needed now was time to make a rational assessment.

Again, he checked his watch. He'd have to rush to get to class. Storefronts seemed to offer cryptic clues as he serpentined through traffic. B. Dalton Books. Tower Records. Hadn't there been a southern Senator once named Towers? A diminutive Lieutenant Dalton in his outfit? No amount of frantic fiddling with the dial settled the radio on one wavelength. The rows of clouds, previously stationary, began to move.

Though several minutes late, he had calmed down by the time he reached the faculty parking lot. But on the steps of Marion Hall he was gripped by a sense of renewed urgency and took them two at a time, before being nearly struck by the heavy wooden door shoved open by an unrepentant coed. The near miss jarred loose a fragile memory.

We know their identities already, Captain. From you we only require verification. Bernard Chodorow . . .

His testimony had come at a price. It was true that the committee knew the names already, many of them men and women like himself, coaxed into attending meetings at an impressionable age, who quickly had grown disenchanted. The tension from those times was like a solvent eating away at his and Madeline's marriage. Before he met Rebecca he'd started drinking, and it afflicted him periodically throughout his career, ebbing and flowing in inverse proportion, ironically, to the success of his latest project. Once after a rare critically acclaimed opening, a script girl found him passed out next to a dumpster in the studio alley. When a therapist recommended a hobby, he took up watercolors. During stretches on the wagon, his anger invariably flared, no doubt contributing to his reputation as a difficult director to work with. It might explain why he eventually stopped receiving offers, and why he'd been reduced in recent years exclusively to teaching.

When he entered the classroom, everyone was seated except three students huddled together by the blackboard. He detected in their sudden stiffness a trace of embarrassment, as if he had caught them gossiping, likely about him. As they found their seats, he took one too, in the back row.

"Begin," he said.

His teaching assistant had already lined up the projector to the sequence up for review, this one from a tired period piece called *Tennessee* set during the Depression. We are midway through and the protagonist, seen from behind, glances around furtively before entering a gigantic barn, where the farmer's lustful daughter awaits. An awkward cut to the hayloft reveals the young woman's hidden brother, spying. Wash felt a short flutter.

"Who is that actor?" he asked in the dark, allowing his pen to roll to the floor. "The one in the loft."

The student whose film they were viewing spoke the name, just another struggling unknown. But Wash experienced the same niggling sense of recognition as he did about the man on the bus, even though this actor was clearly not the same person, he had a narrower face and more menacing eyes. Still seen from behind, the protagonist removes his shirt while standing over the half-naked vixen. Another cut to the loft. The sly brother peeks from behind a beam. Wash couldn't shake the sensation that he knew this man. All of a sudden, a pang in his gut doubled him over. He looked up, perspiring, at the brother gazing down.

"Stop!" he yelled.

He winced at the alarmed students' screeching chairs, which seemed to him somehow coordinated in their disharmony. The T.A. clicked off the projector with a rattle.

"I'm sorry," Wash said. The darkness felt as if it had mass. All seventeen students had turned in his direction. In their dim, curious expressions he saw only evidence of foreboding. He pulled himself together. "Turn on the lights, I'm sorry."

He rose. "I've been . . ." he began. He wanted to cry. He tried again. "How . . . how could this scene have been edited better?"

No one spoke, or moved. He searched their faces until he found one that looked sympathetic, a boy with parted blond hair who resembled a kindly private from his old unit.

"Mr. Kavanaugh," he murmured.

The student tightened the muscles in his neck and turned from side to side. The others glanced around inquiringly.

"Steven Kavanaugh," he said, louder this time.

"Me, sir?"

"Yes, you." The young man's hesitancy was disconcerting. In a life-or-death situation it could cost lives.

"My name is Armstrong, sir. Jeremy Armstrong."

Wash clasped his right hand with his left to keep from shaking. "Of course." He started to sit down. "Of course, I'm sorry. On second thought, why don't we watch a little more before we begin our analysis. Lights. Camera. . . . I'm sorry. Projector."

The film resumed. As the couple begins to kiss and grope, the camera dollies back to reveal an old man wearing overalls in the foreground. He is the woman's overly restrictive father, we know from an earlier scene, and he's holding a pitchfork. Hearing him, the protagonist jumps to his feet. When the student needlessly cuts to a close-up of the frightened younger man, Wash poked his head forward in disbelief.

No, he thought. It can't be him. He killed himself twenty years ago!

Frederick Orr, A.L. Bruckner . . .

The actor playing the lead breaks the fourth wall. He stares directly at the camera, with deep-set eyes strikingly similar to Wash's.

"What is going on here?" Wash said, but too quiet for anyone to notice. He rubbed his neck and swallowed. That actor should be attending to the threat at the barn door!

Next, the young woman playing the daughter, who has sat up in the hay, turns toward camera, as does the actor portraying the old man, whose mineral green eyes seem like an older version of the lead's. It's as if the director cried *Cut!* except no one speaks or walks into frame. The actors narrow their gaze, at Wash in particular, as though considering a decree or gathering data from an experiment.

"Why don't you cut?" This time they all heard him, he could tell by how they stirred. Are they ignoring him? Why doesn't the director yell cut? *Cut!* He wants to yell it himself, to put an end to these undisciplined actors glaring at him in this shameless manner. *Cut!*

"Cut!"

His aide snapped off the projector. Someone flipped on the lights. He took a deep breath, relieved. After a full minute of silence, someone said, "Sir, are you all right?"

"I'm fine," he said, his eyes fixed on the blank screen. He put a palm to his forehead. "Put it back on, soldier."

The student and the aide looked sideways at each other. "Well? Put it on!"

On screen the tyrannical old farmer and the young stud do battle over control of the pitchfork, as the farmer's daughter, literally licking her lips, and the son in the loft, mimicking the young man's moves, watch in wide-eyed anticipation of a bloody end to their oppression. Wash's jaw muscles tensed. He gripped the desk. One of the lines blurred between past and present, reality and fiction. He rushed to the front, pulled up the screen.

"No!" he yelled, when the T.A. shut off the movie. "Turn it on. Your actors have broken the fourth wall, Mr. Kavanaugh," he scolded. The film played around and upon him, revealing and obscuring his face in patches of light and shadow. He began to write words on the blackboard, difficult to make out in the flickering glow.

The T.A. stood up as if to object but returned to his seat when Wash glanced at him sharply. He assumed they had all heard the stories. God knows his little *episodes* had become the subject of enough chatter in the faculty lounge. The arrest for drunk driving in Monterey Park. The suspension following a brawl on the football field with a post-doc in political science.

He focused again on what he was writing. "You can use these men," he said. "Good men."

They were names he inscribed. Outdated names, some of them frustratingly familiar:

Elmer Tottle
ADrian Koestler
Orson JerRico

Over them the old farmer wrestles the pitchfork free and rushes at his opponent. Wash's arm moved mechanically as he crossed out some names but not others.

> Ben Wolpe
> ~~john SampSon Tatz~~

"Disappeared," or "Left town," or "Dead," he'd say over individual deletions. "Actors, directors, screenwriters." He spoke without facing the class. "They will work cheap," he said, oblivious to the movie. "They *need* the work."

On screen the younger man sidesteps and tackles his elder, the pitchfork landing at their feet. He hurts his arm in the fall, and the farmer, holding a momentary advantage, raises a metal fence post over his head to deal the death blow. . . .

Another line blurred. Wash put down names in a panic now, no longer in neat columns. He allowed them to bleed into one another or set them apart, angled or emboldened them, some of which were nonsensical or of non-people and of tenebrous origins, like a child rearranging letters in a dream.

> Ararat   Mont ag Ne
> KrAHN   ~~Fenton~~ (gone)   *Der* p   **Ad**
> P al wic k   **gsw** *vsekh*   Anzrs   ~~*derley*~~

"Enough?" he cried, scribbling incoherently. From his knees the Lothario is able to secure the pitchfork and fatally jab the old farmer. Scott Randol, the shyest member of class, was the one to finally interrupt.

"Mr. Washevsky," he said. "Sir, we have to go. It's time."

"Dismissed," he said, without abandoning his mission. "Congratulations, gentlemen. Ladies. You have done your duty as Americans."

The board was almost full as they got up to leave, whispering like judges. No one dared turn off the projector or turn on the lights. Minutes later Professor Denkins stepped in after peering through the glass.

"Wash? Are you all right?"

Wash mumbled something but kept fitting more names onto the board.

"Wash?" He flicked off the projector. Only when he put on the lights did Wash become fully conscious of the intrusion. "Wash, stop that." He placed a hand on his shoulder.

Wash pivoted sharply and gasped, at his colleague's eyes and the enemy they reflected. He raised an arm as if to strike but Denkins grabbed it. "Wash! For *Chrissake*, snap out of it!"

In pulling away, Wash knocked over a chair. He fell to the floor and slid back into a corner, all the while moving his lips in fast motion and looking up in terror, as if his associate were an SS guard or one of Stalin's henchmen, or Satan's messenger on earth. The lights went off on a timer. Denkins shook his head and sighed as he reached for the door, knowing there would be another report, and probably some kind of tribunal.

Government

My next-door neighbor Farley and I don't speak to each other. Two years ago, he installed a wood-burning fireplace in his living room, and the fumes from it circulate through my house when the wind blows from the northwest. When standing on his porch I informed him of that fact, he responded from the darkness behind his chained front door that the chimney was up to code, so fuck off.

Farley is a man of few words. His preferred form of communication is symbols. On St. Patrick's Day he flies an Irish flag up the pole on his front lawn. On Washington's Birthday it's the Sons of Liberty. When a Black woman and her son moved into the neighborhood, for a week he had placed at the end of his walkway a ceramic planter containing one large and one small boll of cotton.

I think Farley thinks of himself as a good neighbor. He shovels the elderly couple's driveway across the alley when it snows. He keeps his lawn and elaborate garden expertly manicured. Every Saturday in spring he washes his pickup truck, which has a license plate that reads DUTY1. His vintage green tractor is immaculate.

Yes, he keeps a tractor in his garage, a John Deere circa 1940. Once in a while he takes it for a slow trip around our suburban neighborhood and waves to people as he passes. Sometimes he's waving even when no one is there. When he's waving and driving his old tractor is the only time I've seen him smile. He isn't a farmer. Until recently he worked a graveyard shift at the weapons plant.

To me, Farley has been anything but a good neighbor. In addition to the chimney episode, he periodically encroaches on my property in ways that are insignificant by themselves but in the aggregate rise to the level of provocation. Early in every campaign season, for instance, he sets up an oversized sign on his front lawn just an inch or two from my lot in support of the most anti-government candidate. In back, without consulting me, he planted rosebushes along the property line, and when he cuts his lawn around them, he includes an eight-by-ten-foot patch of grass that is clearly part of my land—not, I think, for the same reason he shovels the Edgars' driveway, but because the length I let the grass grow, although well within the normal range, disturbs him, and he's secretly hoping I'll confront him about the mowing so that he can disapprove in person of my perceived lack of industry.

I got an idea for the source of Farley's anger one day when his parents arrived for a visit while I was working in the yard. He greeted them at the curb and tried to help his father, who has trouble walking.

"I can *do* it," the father snapped, wresting his arm from Farley's grasp. Farley's acquiescent nod suggested his father's response was not an unfamiliar one. "If you want to be useful, make sure the table is set proper for your mother this time," his father instructed.

Over the next week or two, I heard examples of Farley becoming bolder than ever in his demands for conformity and order. He gave two thumbs down and a raspberry to a friend of mine leaving our house after a dinner party: a reaction, as my friend was informed after challenging Farley about it, to the COEXIST bumper sticker on his Volvo. Another day my wife heard him yell "Shut up, damn dog!" at our poodle for briefly barking in the backyard. Later that week, Farley called the police about the dog. We were told by the embarrassed cop who gave us the warning that Roxie had allegedly been barking while we were out. She'd been inside her kennel in the house at the time. The woman who lives on the other side of us told us later that she'd seen Farley from her porch stop his yard work that day and stand at the property line scowling for close to an hour, tightly gripping his weed eater, intently listening to the dog's intermittent barking behind our closed curtains, which was almost inaudible from where she sat.

One evening I'd had about enough. It was late May, I remember, when I discovered that Farley had stuck a trellis in the ground on my parcel, where the fence turns at a right angle onto my half of the strip of land between our homes. He had planted a clematis vine that was growing up the trellis and fence and spilling into my backyard. That night I removed the plant, along with the trellis, and tossed them onto the walkway bisecting Farley's front lawn.

The next morning was Memorial Day. Farley must have worked the previous night and come home through the garage or else I'm sure he would have noticed the trellis and removed it. I was on the porch reading the paper, steeling for a confrontation, when Farley's family arrived. This time he failed to meet his parents at the curb. And this time they were accompanied by a younger man I guessed to be Farley's brother, who helped his father out of the car without any resistance. Pinned to the father's shirt were three medals that glistened in the bright sun. When he and his son got to the walkway, they noticed the vine and trellis in their path and stopped. The father shook his head like a man whose faith in controversial beliefs had been vindicated. At that moment Farley came bursting out the front door. The father looked up and Farley froze, stiffened by fear.

"Case in point of what I been saying, Bennett," the father said to his other son. "Any self-respecting man keeps his things in their proper place."

"What happened, Farley?" the brother teased. "A tornado come on up through here?" He chuckled as he helped his father around the uprooted vine. Farley moved out of the way and kept silent. When his family was inside, he gathered up the plant and was hurrying around back with it when he noticed me, and glared as if I had just set fire to his home.

* * *

That was the next-to-last time I saw Farley. I did hear stories about his subsequent frenzy of intolerance. Outside the polls at a special election the following month, he got in the face of a man running for state representative and had to be escorted away by authorities. A week later, while driving his truck, he clipped the rearview mirror of a parked car owned by a Latina looking at houses in our development. She saw it happen, ran outside, and followed him home. On his front porch she received a similar response to the one I got when I complained about the smoke.

Before long the intensity Farley brought to his politics and personal habits found a pathway to his brain: he suffered a severe stroke. As he was not the type to neglect to call in to work, when he didn't show up or phone, his supervisor sent a man looking. It was early morning by the time the ambulance arrived. Several of us neighbors heard the sirens and came outside to investigate. While they were loading him in, his mother drove up alone. I don't think she made herself known or I'm sure they would have let her ride with her son to the hospital. Instead, as it drove off, she watched from the middle of the street, hunched over and bowlegged, clutching a rosary.

Farley won't be working for a while. He's in a wheelchair now. His speech is slurred and he goes to therapy three times a week to relearn how to walk and talk, a recovery that could take years. He lives with his mother and father on the farm. She feeds him and makes sure he does his exercises, and every month he receives a disability check from the government he loathes.

Skinny Dugan

The End

The final time I entered the casino, my pockets were empty except for keys and a hundred and fifty dollars I'd stolen from Party, what everyone called my then-wife Partridge, whose real name was Jane. A roar greeted me at the entrance—the roar of hot dice.

A gambler's superstitions are sacrosanct. In craps it's bad luck when a player gets hit by the dice because he's bending into the layout to pick up chips or to make a bet while the dice are in the air. Just as bad is a shooter who can't consistently get the dice to the end of the table. I also believed, with considerable anecdotal evidence to back me up, that you don't enter a game in the middle of a good roll.

"Fifteen-minute roll, Felix. You getting in?"

I knew most of the dealers, most of the addicts. But the players on this game were unfamiliar. Poker players sitting out a string of bad cards. A couple out for a night on the town. The shooter, a bald man wearing a leather bomber jacket, took his time, set the dice carefully, and lofted them each throw with an identical arc.

"Six, a winner," the stickman declared. "Nothing but winners."

Twenty more minutes passed, number after number, the same precise ritual from the shooter.

"Felix, you're not going to sit out this whole roll, are you?"

Fucking dealers, my God.

"One-thirty-seven across," I said, finally giving in, and, significantly, announcing it while simultaneously leaning over the table to set my chips in the Come.

"Bet!"

It happened that the shooter abandoned his routine just then for some reason, or for no reason at all, and quick-threw the dice, which hit me in the shoulder and for the first time failed to reach the end of the table.

"Seven out!" the stickman cried when they landed in the Field. "Line 'em in."

A chorus of moans followed. Like the moans one imagines from the faceless damned in a painting by Hieronymus Bosch.

"Jesus," one man moaned.

"Watch it! Oh, Christ!"

Line 'em in. Everyone loses.

It goes without saying.

I sarcastically tipped the dealers the thirteen bucks I had left, and that was the end of my gambling.

Rain

In winter, a light rain never seemed to let up until it wasn't rain anymore, but a mockery of rain, the way time to a prisoner becomes nothing more than an empty calendar.

Winning

The jolly rich fat man in charge of building the downtown stadium was the first catalyst of my addiction. A big tipper, a one-hour roll, a woman, literally, on each arm. And laughing the whole time, yakking it up. Thousands of dollars in play. Everyone had the time of their lives, high-fiving strangers. I walked away two grand up, and even though I stumbled in horny and drunk at six a.m., my girlfriend at the time couldn't stay mad at me long, once I spread out all that money.

Dance

Today you associate ballroom dance with former athletes and television stars engaged in some humiliating spectacle, so desperate are they to recapture their fifteen minutes of fame. Back then it meant whatever remained of Arthur Murray and its progeny, or what your grandparents did for romance before God invented rock 'n' roll. One of those offspring was Ted Blaine's Dance Club, where I found myself employed after answering a classified ad.

Compensation

A typical member of the club might be a seventy-three-year-old widow—a Beatrice or a Minnie or a Gladys—women with names so outdated that not changing them became a kind of passive rebellion against the tyranny of obsolescence. Another type was a middle-aged couple in a stale marriage who weren't ready to acknowledge their troubles openly yet but sensed them, so that when our flyer came in the mail with a free lesson, the wife, understanding on some level their need for a fresh start, would suggest they try it out, and after an argument of whatever length, depending on whether he had someone on the side yet, the husband would give in, calculating the pain from an hour of swing and cha-cha to be less than the price of smoldering acrimony. The last type consisted of young, single women. These usually had obvious physical shortcomings—weight issues, many of them, or simply below-average looks. One of mine had curly red hair and stood six foot seven. Waltzing, we looked like rejects from the world's worst circus.

I ended up there after being fired from my sales job at a for-profit college for stealing. I did it; I took the money in order to gamble. I was a pretty good salesman—*marketer* is the term they used there—but even so, the commissions weren't enough to satisfy my habit. In the new position, the ability to dance was not a prerequisite. I answered the ad because I sensed a secret sales job in it, and I was right. As long as you could stay a couple lessons ahead of your beginner students you were okay, the idea being to keep things light and build trust, enough to sell them bigger packages down the road, some of which ran as much as fifteen *G*s. The owners, a born huckster with a pockmarked face and his wife, a relentlessly positive, wide-eyed former student of his, were like the people at the college, only preying on the lonely instead of the stupid and the poor.

The dance club occupied a large, mirrored space in the basement of a mall on the outskirts of Seattle. The main floor housed a food court where you could buy falafel from an Indonesian, tempura from a transplanted Valley girl, or spaghetti and meatballs from a taciturn Sikh. Occasionally I hit on the Croatian woman who made the burritos, a refugee from the Yugoslav Wars. Her quiet dignity put me to shame. In her homeland she might have been the leader of some arcane resistance movement known only by its initials. In the food court she folded tortillas and rejected my advances.

On the way home I would stop at the casino in Tulalip. After I finally lost everything and started going to Gamblers Anonymous, I still stopped there but I didn't go in, I just sat in my car in the parking lot, sometimes as long as an hour, testing my resolve. One night after a party at the club, at which I'd lugged around a cranky old widow named Hazel for over an hour in the hopes of selling her a Bronze program, and after which, with the help of the owner's remarkable closing skills, we did sell her that program, resulting in a substantial commission for me, my resolve wavered. Fortunately, the party went late, and I had stayed up so late the night before to personalize Hazel's program, describing the many ways that dancing would benefit her hardened octogenarian soul, that I was exhausted and fell asleep in my car at the casino before the decision could be made as to whether to risk my not-yet-posted commission on baccarat, roulette, or dice. I woke to the slam of a car door. Across from me, entering her car from the wet night was a dealer at the end of her shift, a woman who had dealt blackjack to me many times. She didn't notice me, or pretended not to. Her name was Sandra Lacy, and I'd hated her from the first night she cleaned me out.

Don't get me wrong, with obsessive gamblers it's never about money. I hated her because of her attitude. She wanted to win. She dealt fast and made comments that seemed harmless on the surface, but in a mocking tone: "Oh, I guess you shouldn't have hit that." "Can't win tonight, can you?" "Nineteen, that's good," and then, revealing her own hand, "Oops, twenty. Not good eno-ough," drawing out the final word into two syllables like that, almost singing it, as she swiped away my losing bet.

I never beat her, and I believe she was proud of that. Several times as I walked away busted, I looked back to see if she was laughing at me, a snub I never witnessed but always sensed lurking behind a barely suppressed smile. A Native American like many of the dealers, she had long black hair she wore swept around her neck, and a face that was easy to look at despite a vague indication of gloom. The casino sat on a reservation, overseen by the council of the Tulalip Tribes. Presumably they were among the myriad tribes we'd stolen land from and were now paying back by granting licenses to steal. Another quarter of the dealers were Southeast Asian—Laotians or Cambodians or Vietnamese—the children of refugees, displaced souls, who, along with the Natives, gambled disproportionally in their off-hours. As for Sandra, I had nowhere to go, so I followed her out of there with some dim notion of confronting her when she got home.

We only had to drive a few minutes. It was past midnight, moonless, overcast. I followed her down a gravel road into a trailer park, past a group of Natives drinking around a fire. A quarter mile beyond them, she pulled up next to a trailer and parked beneath a frilled awning. I drove past it a couple hundred yards, turned off my lights, and waited. Then I skulked back to do whatever it was I intended—assault her in some way, I think, looking back on it, if she'd been alone and I'd been able to muster up the courage.

In the distance the Natives' voices commingled with the crackle of fire. A light turned on as I approached her trailer. On tiptoes I could see her through half-drawn curtains exit a small bedroom. I waited, alternately looking toward the park entrance while affecting a nonchalant pose and rising up in anticipation of her return. The smell of wet trees reminded me of childhood fears. When she finally did return, her hair was damp. She wore a towel that covered her breasts and hips, but just barely.

She unfastened the towel and threw it onto a chair in my direction. At that angle, I could tell I was invisible to her, a shadow among shadows. She removed a silken, cream-colored chemise from a drawer, a striking indulgence in those surroundings. Her naked body revealed a tattoo of an eagle on her hip, with a white-feathered cap straining toward her belly. My desire for revenge merged with sexual longing. I heard primal screams and saw the luscious earth before the dawn of man. She put on the garment and got into bed, and I walked to the other side of the trailer in front of the door, where I weighed whether to take back in one fiendish act everything I believed I was owed.

Who contemplates something like that? Me back then, that's who. I stood there for what might have been seconds or hours, with the same rush I felt after pulling the arm of a slot machine waiting for the wheels to turn. I was about to knock when out of the darkness, staggering in my direction and mumbling to himself, approached a man. I don't know if he saw me. I hustled to my car. I do know, by looking back from the top of the road, that he—her husband or boyfriend or some braver offender than I—entered her trailer.

At home, in bed, I wrote false assurances in half-finished programs. The Rosenquists would learn proper spacing for their upcoming showcase. Carrie Anne would express the romance she craves through the magic of sway.

Playing

I am not the only villain in my own story. I felt justified stealing the money from my wife, for instance, from the stash I knew she kept under bras and panties in her bureau, because a month before that I'd come home early from the dance club and walked in on her *in flagrante delicto*, as they say, like the flash point in some big-box-office movie. The guy had worked on the furnace. His name was Frank. I didn't interrupt them. I went straight to the casino and had the night of my life. I bet the Player hand at baccarat eight times in a row and it came up Player every time. For the first hour after I got home, I forgot that I'd been cuckolded. To be honest, I didn't much care. I never confronted Partridge about it, even later that spring, when after eighteen months of marriage we put an end to our charade.

Color

Sometime after the break-up I started seeing an Asian woman who had begun working at the club. She was half-Korean. The other half Slovenian or Slovakian or something. Built like an Olympic wrestler. She wore boots everywhere, an extraordinary variety: army boots, go-go boots, Uggs. She kept her hair in a kind of mohawk, buzz cut on the sides, long in the middle. Two nights a week she stripped at a club called the Blue Lady Lounge, and the rest of the week, like me, she taught lonely hearts how to shuffle around a dance floor.

We started grabbing a drink after work and soon we were having sex. What a fireball! Twice we got kicked out of dives because she sassed back at some lippy drunk woman and refused to quiet down. I always stayed out of it. She brought that same passion to the bedroom, although I detected a note of insincerity in her loud cries, a carryover, I guessed, from the false interest demanded of her at her other vocation. In those days I didn't sleep much. I spent a lot of time smoking and drinking, walking around town, reading obituaries and want ads. What I liked best about her, believe it or not, was that she maintained a beautiful garden. She grew blackberries, tomatoes—and the flowers! Her colorful front yard shouted WAKE UP, QUITTERS to a neglectful neighborhood. Unfortunately, her tenure at the club came to an abrupt end. She had just begun teaching me to cook when at our meeting the next day, the owner, who did not appreciate her rawness the way I did, called her out for being repeatedly late, knowing what her reaction would be. She flipped him off and walked out, much to the pleasure of the owner's wife, in particular. That might have been the last time I saw her. This was before cell phones were commonplace. I'm not sure we'd even exchanged home numbers.

Deceit

Around that time, a gambler I used to see periodically on a blackjack game started showing up at G.A. meetings. The dealers knew him as the guy who came in twice a day for an hour, first at five a.m. wearing a running outfit, and then again in the evening, always in a suit. He'd been keeping his gambling a secret from his wife, telling her that he was working late each night and jogging in the mornings. He told me that one of the dealers we both liked, a kid named Charlie Freed, had been arrested. This kid had remarkable hands, a real magician. It turns out that for months he'd been making one black chip—a hundred dollars—disappear from his tray every night, somehow getting it into his mouth without being detected. That would explain why Charlie, so friendly by nature, would occasionally go silent for as much as an hour at a time. They finally caught him on a night he was coming down with a cold. A stolen chip rolled across the dice pit and landed at the shift manager's feet as Charlie was walking to break, after he suddenly and uncontrollably sneezed.

Darkness

Night after night I returned to the casino just before Sandra Lacy ended her shift. I parked near the exit, watched her get into her car, and followed her home. I had no reason to follow since I knew where she lived and could have waited for her there. But the process exhilarated me, the simulated chase. The routine helped me formulate what it was I was doing.

Which was what, exactly? I don't know what I envisioned originally. Knocking on her door, stepping inside. Eventually I imagined her naked, backed up against the refrigerator. I would demand sex, to which she would fold her arms and refuse even to respond. That's where the fantasy got a little murky. We would have sex. Not consensual sex but not rape, either. I know that isn't possible given the legal niceties of it. It's a fantasy! Suspend disbelief. Her ultimate acquiescence was a key part of our reckoning, in my mind. The fantasy always degenerated from there into some twisted reverse humiliation, when during the act she'd begin to make flippant comments similar to the ones she made on the tables: "Not good eno-ough," all singsong, or "Having a little trouble tonight?"

Or: "So sad, you've come up short again."

The truth is I was too fragile to make any part of my vision a reality, thank God. Each night, I rolled down that gravel road and turned past what seemed like the same circle of darkly clad men drinking around a fire. I parked in the recess of a pine grove at the top of the hill and snuck back to the modest place that Sandra Lacy called home. Since at least one set of curtains was always open, I always peeked in.

Sometimes, as on the first night, I caught a glimpse of her in the nude. Other nights she changed clothes out of view, and I was only able to observe her tidying up or watching television. It always ended the same, with the same man wobbling up the path, visibly drunk even from a distance. I learned the rhythms of his approach so well that I never failed to get out of there in time. I never got a good look at his face. Instead, I would watch him from a distance, wait a few minutes after he entered the unlocked trailer, and drive away.

On the seventh night, it all happened the same until the end. As I was putting my key in the ignition, I thought I saw a small object inside the trailer zip in and out of view. Before I could question whether it was a trick of the moon's light, a sound of shattering glass made me shudder. A plate or a cup maybe striking a wall, it was followed immediately by the muffled voice of the man yelling. On some level, I'd known this was coming. Their living conditions, his habitual drinking, her subtle expressions of contempt, all made an eruption of violence feel inevitable. In retrospect, it's what I'd been waiting for all along, for this mysterious man to take my revenge for me. I heard from Sandra Lacy what sounded like pleas. I could not make out words, even the man's, who again raised his voice. I would not have been ashamed then to admit that I became excited. Images emerged of hunted birds and the ancient settling of scores. I longed to hear her cry out in pain, to beg for mercy, only to be refused.

Their silhouettes drifted behind the curtains like the shadows in some aboriginal play. I decided I needed to witness her comeuppance up close. But as I neared, the figures vanished. At the window I stretched upward and peered into their empty kitchen, where the shards of a broken vase lay scattered on the linoleum floor. The sink faucet had been left running. Hearing voices in the living room, I slid around front intending to try the window on the other side of the door. Just as I passed, it sprung open. I whirled around and froze.

Out stepped the man. He looked older than I'd imagined, with long stringy hair, a rutted face. He didn't see me at first, but when he did, he took a step backward.

"What are you doing here?" he demanded.

"I—"

"Who are you?" His voice had the timbre of a drunken sage.

"I'm lost," I said, beginning the speech I'd prepared for such an occasion. "I turned in here by mistake and can't find my way out."

My explanation appeared to confuse him. He held the railing for a moment to keep from falling.

"I'm looking for the main road."

He ignored me and began wringing his hands. The light from inside revealed that one of his hands had blood on it that was running down his arm. When he finally looked up, we made eye contact.

"I cut myself," he said, holding out his hands. He started to teeter and grabbed the railing again for balance. That's all he said. He hung his head and exhaled hard as I eased around him, saying, "It'll be all right, man. You'll be all right." Before darting up the hill, I took my eyes off him only for an instant, as I passed the screen door and caught a glimpse of Sandra Lacy sweeping up glass.

Trauma

Every day at the club the dance director gave the instructors, many of whom, like me, had no formal training at all, a lesson in grace. This was the best part of the job because I got to pair up with the female instructors, who were invariably young, straight, and attractive, whereas most of the male teachers were gay. Occasionally the numbers didn't match up and I ended up dancing with one of the gay guys. It was awkward at first, but I adapted to it just fine. It only bothered me with this real flamer, a wiry short-timer who wore hair extensions and never stopped talking. He made everyone laugh, especially the women. It was his brash manner more than anything else that we found funny. We even laughed one night after work, at a bar, by the splashy way he told us that he'd been sexually molested as a child by his grandfather. His grandfather! Jocularity! At the time, I wondered if that's what made him turn out gay.

Here's the way it worked: The woman in charge of generating leads lured people in with a free lesson. We "specialists" showed them a few steps, livened it up with our enthusiasm and charm, and sat them down afterward to push a four-lesson program for ninety-nine bucks. If they bought, at the end of their fourth lesson we hit them up again for a $1,500 "Medley" package. A surprising number went for it. Like a ballplayer, if you batted .250 you could make a living; .333 put you in the Hall of Fame. After that came the much bigger Bronze program. Some people also bought showcases: formal choreographed routines they performed with their instructors at annual balls. We offered Silver and Gold programs, too, but almost everyone was tapped out long before that.

Most of the older women didn't care to learn new steps, they just wanted to talk and be led around the floor—or carried, as it often seemed, like with Hazel the Curmudgeon, whose short, Gumby-like frame belied how heavy she felt draped over my arms. I preferred the retired couples where the man had no gracefulness at all. Former blue-collar

workers were best. Give me a retired fireman or lathe opera-
tor, men whose muscles ached and who stopped the lessons
to tell jokes or old stories. One guy I taught, along with his
wife, had engaged in hand-to-hand combat in Vietnam. He
had a nervous tic and frequently glanced around the room
as if anticipating an ambush. The lessons were primarily to
placate his wife; he had no interest in dancing whatsoever.

With not just him, with everyone, over time, listening
to them, getting to know them, I felt less like a teacher of
dance and more like a psychiatrist specializing in PTSD.

Seven

At one of the meetings, we went around the circle and talked
about our favorite games. One guy liked the Big Wheel, a
game with terrible odds that they place by the door to get
your last dollar on the way out. One night in bed he dreamed
of a system that would work on the wheel and hustled to the
casino in his pajamas to get there before it closed. He lost
the last of his bankroll just as they were locking the doors.

The game I miss most is craps, with its scatological name
and its sexually evocative lingo: horn, hard eight, Big Red,
don't come. Knowing its terms makes you feel unflappable,
part of some exclusive fraternity, like you belong.

My favorite piece of jargon is not suggestive at all—it's
Skinny Dugan. People with only a passing familiarity with
craps think that when the dice land on seven it's a good
thing, but that is not usually the case. More often than not,
a seven means the shooter is done and everyone loses. A
player saying the word seven on a game is therefore considered bad luck, so various alternative names have evolved,
one of which is Skinny Dugan. It's a way of saying, without

actually saying, what you hope won't happen but know will eventually come.

Grace

Why would I return to the trailer park after the encounter I'd had, with a drunk and potentially dangerous Native American? It's a fair question. Which I answer with a question: What else did I have now that I'd sworn off my favored form of risk?

I wanted to be there when the tension escalated, to witness the woman's lover exact the revenge I was too cowardly to claim. I wondered if, and on whose behalf, I would intervene.

I returned several times but saw nothing to indicate conflict. Finally, one night from my car I noticed the light in the camper shimmer and then dim, as if a lamp had been knocked to the floor. The shout of a man was replaced by a female cry. I approached stealthily, stopping when the light grew full again, the lamp set straight. I began to hear echoes of struggle and reproach. The kitchen window was shut, so I went around back to the one farthest from the door, my plan in the event of another surprise meeting to simply flee, a plan derived from my calculation that the man, in our prior encounter, had seemed more preoccupied than threatening, and that his age and condition made him unlikely to pursue. A full moon hung low as if to spotlight my shamelessness. Again, the curtains were parted; the closed windows dampened the couple's sounds. The yelling intensified and then suddenly stopped. I have never been more excited, not on a one-hour roll, not on a double down at the table maximum.

When I raised up on my toes, what I witnessed confused me. The woman wasn't there. Face down on the couch lay the man, his body convulsing. What had I missed? Was he hurt? His hand was heavily bandaged. Had he assaulted his lover—his wife?—and left her for dead in the kitchen?

I craned in an effort to see more, but there was nothing to see; the woman was gone. I decided that the man wasn't hurt, he was sobbing, and the bandage was most likely the result of his outburst the week before. Then, suddenly, from below, Sandra Lacy stood into view on the opposite side of the pane.

". . . air might help," I heard her say, as she slid open the window.

It happened too quickly for me to react. We were close enough to play cards. Had she looked out she would have seen me, but her head was turned.

"I'll get you some water," she said before heading to the kitchen.

When she returned, she sat on the couch and helped him sit up. I was right, he had been crying. Now he was breathing deeply, his eyes as black as graves. He drank from the glass. She stroked his hair. After a long pause, he sighed and said, "She's gone."

He began to cry again, softly. She cradled his head and teared up also. "I know, daddy," she said finally. "I miss her too."

I had not noticed in my prior confrontation with him how much they looked alike. "She fought hard," I heard her say very faintly. Her father nodded, his eyes focused on the paneled wall, where for the first time I noticed a framed picture of a Native American woman about his age standing by a river, smiling.

"She's with the angels now," the man said, staring at the woman I presumed to be his late wife.

Hoping for violence, I'd confused mourning with rage. Suddenly violence seemed as unlikely in that setting as hitting the lottery or developing some rare disease. I never prayed, but when I finally settled to the ground, I prayed for forgiveness. At home, splashing water on my face, I had trouble looking in the mirror.

Greta

One of my students at that time had suffered a traumatic brain injury. Her name was Greta. She'd been on the back of a motorcycle with the on-again, off-again boyfriend she intended to break up with for good that night when an accident killed him. She must have been twenty-four or twenty-five. She moved in with her parents afterward, who thought dancing might be good therapy for her depression. She got around pretty well except for a slight limp, and she talked almost like a regular person except that her short-term memory was shot, so she often repeated herself. She had that faraway, brain-damaged look in her eyes, like a gentle zombie.

Because she tired easily, we would frequently cut her lessons short and just talk at one of the tables. She liked to tell stories about her family. When she was a teenager, her grandfather showed up without her grandmother once at a holiday gathering and wouldn't say why. Nobody asked. That's what kind of family they were, very German. They acted like it was normal and only talked about her grandmother's absence in whispers in secluded corners. The grandmother—her father's mother—later asked her father how to go about getting a divorce. Her father shrugged it off, and his parents stayed unhappily married until they died a week apart from each other several years later. Long before Greta was born, the grandfather had briefly placed the grandmother in a sanatorium where she received shock therapy, but no one talked about that either, she said. I got the impression that Greta used to hold things close to the chest too, but the injury changed all that, much to her family's ongoing bewilderment.

Those first lessons we ran out of time before we wanted them to end, so we started meeting outside of the club. Nothing sexual. We'd meet in coffee shops, drink lattes, eat scones. The injury had left her with a heightened sense of smell, and she found the aromas there especially pleasing. She'd help me tailor Medley programs to particular clients by suggesting alternative words for my descriptions. She'd been an English major in college and had a large vocabulary. "Write *festive* instead of *fun*," she'd say, or "*Nimble* works better than *graceful* there." Then, forgetting what she'd said, a few minutes later she'd repeat it: "*Festive* sounds better than *fun*, don't you think?"

When it came time to sell her a Medley program, she knew what was going on. I was perfectly honest about our procedures. "I'm brain damaged, not stupid," she said. She bought the whole package. In the closing room, she told the owner she wanted to buy even before he opened his mouth.

A week later she didn't show up for her first Medley lesson. A middle-aged woman came in when the lesson was scheduled to begin and demanded to talk to the owner. Through his glass office wall, I watched her lean in and angrily point an index finger into his desk. It turned out to be Greta's mother. When she learned that Greta had paid $1,500 for dance lessons, she assumed we'd taken advantage of her daughter's disability. The owner refunded their money. I called Greta at home several times in the days that followed. Each time, her mother picked up and refused to let Greta talk. The final time, she threatened to call the police.

The Beginning

My grouchy, eighty-one-year-old client Hazel had been a cop—twenty-eight years on the force followed by seventeen as a prison guard at the women's penitentiary. I learned that during the first of the two hundred Bronze lessons she purchased to while away her retirement. She hated that word, *retirement*; it intimated of death. She couldn't remember my name, but she remembered that I used to gamble, so she called me Lucky. Whenever I told her a story about some degenerate gambler, or started in about the depths to which I myself had sunk in my darkest days, she'd say something like, "You think that's grim, Lucky? You don't know what grim is."

Life is so damn sad when you stare it in the face without blinking. Only when you see the sadness in others can you put your own in the proper perspective.

I stuck with that job for two years and had only one relapse, a brief night of roulette inspired by gin-induced madness. I lost, thank God. Mostly, it's a period I look back on fondly, when I began to feel, even if most of what I felt was regret. The dancing made a big difference. Who would have thought that an old witch, a TBI victim, a jittery Vietnam vet, and all the rest could play a part in my recovery, or me in theirs, just by propping each other up and shambling from one end of a room to the other?

King Kong

It's early in the shift on a busy night at the casino. The pencil has scheduled me on my own blackjack table, where I'm shuffling cards when King Kong walks up.

"Is third base open?" he asks.

"All yours, Thanh."

Third base is slang for the seat on the dealer's far right. Some players prefer it because the third baseman is the last one to take a hit before the dealer plays her cards, so his decisions appear to affect the game more than anyone else's. In fact, that's an illusion: all players' decisions affect the outcome equally, it's just that the last player's choices are the ones everyone remembers.

"Ok?" Thanh asks, looking at the other players at the table. They nod or shrug and he takes a seat on the end. Thanh is a regular blackjack player. He runs a Vietnamese restaurant with his family.

"You hot?" he asks me.

Another man says, "She's a bad girl."

"She's tearing me a new asshole," says the guy sitting between them.

I tell Thanh I think the cards will change now that he's here, and he smiles. "I play good third base," he says to the other players. "Dealers know me."

Then I start dealing.

Right off the bat he gets a chance to prove himself. On the first hand I have a four showing. The others have nineteen or twenty and stand pat. Thanh has twelve.

"I stay," he says, waving his hand over his cards. "Let dealer bust."

I flip my hole card, a queen, giving me fourteen. When I'm about to take another card, as the rules require, Thanh yells "Big monkey!" That's his thing. I turn over a jack and bust. Everybody wins. As I'm paying out, Thanh says to the others, "Game changing now. Have good third baseman."

He never tips. I can tell it's going to be a long night.

* * *

"I saw King Kong on your game," Arlene says when I'm walking to break. "Lucky you."

My breaks coincide with Wyatt's, who's running a relief string. He's watching a football game with Rachelle, which is too bad because I was hoping to finish the talk we had the night before about expenses, who pays for what when, now that he's all moved in.

"That's going to leave a mark," he says to the TV when a player gets hit in the chest with a guy's helmet. Rachelle laughs. She's actually interested in sports, she isn't just pretending.

* * *

You have to be able to put things in perspective, what it all means.

Back on the game, I lose concentration for a second and make a mistake, hitting a player's hand who's signaled he wants to stick. Easy to fix. I call over the supervisor. He has me burn the card.

"Change order of cards," Thanh says. "No good."

"Maybe it'll change them for the better," I say, trying to be sensible. Thanh looks at me like my head is made out of glass.

The game goes cold for a while. Players come and go. Thanh keeps shaking his head, mumbling under his breath.

Then that well-dressed kid walks up, the one who likes to flirt.

"Don't sit," says Thanh. "She hot."

"That's why I'm here," he says, taking a seat. "Because she's hot."

I say, "Where you been lately, Gio?" I can feel myself smiling.

"Oh, out and about. You lose some weight since the last time I saw you? You look great in that uniform."

My night is picking up. On break, Leslie says something about my handsome young admirer. When I peek into the smoking break room, Rachelle isn't there, but I don't talk to Wyatt. He's moaning at the TV and rolling his eyes, disgusted. "Of course he throws an interception," he says to himself. It's near the end of some big game or something. I know when not to mess with Wyatt.

The players start to win when I get back. On the last hand of a shoe, Thanh does what he did earlier, he stands pat hoping I'll draw the bust card. This time he yells "King Kong!" It's so loud that everyone in our pit can hear it. I bust, and the whole table gives out a little cheer. Thanh gets up on his soapbox while I shuffle.

"People play crazy," he says. "I can win you if people don't play crazy. Believe me. You know how I play. I good third baseman. I follow my feeling. Dealer bust last hand, don't split seven. That crazy. Change cards."

"I see your point," I say, but I don't really see it.

A woman on the game says, "I believe if you're lucky then you'll win; if you're not, you won't. That's what I believe."

"Ask anyone," Thanh says, not listening. "I know this game. I play every day. I make dealer bust if people not come in and out. Ask dealer. I play good third base. I lose fifty, seventy thousand dollars here, no problem. Play every day. You tell them."

"Thanh is very experienced," I confirm to the table.

"That's the word," says Thanh. "I experience."

Under his breath, Gio says, "You sure the word isn't *sucker?*"

I shoot him a conspiratorial glance. He's sitting on first base, so I don't think Thanh heard him. But Thanh can tell that he said something critical by how we looked at each other, and he stops talking.

During the next shoe, Thanh grumbles every time Gio makes what Thanh considers a bad decision. One time Gio splits nines against my six and Thanh throws up his hands. When it's Thanh's turn, he sticks with thirteen and yells "Big Monkey!" as I draw a ten that puts me over twenty-one.

"I save table," he says, taking credit. "I know. Table hot, don't split." This last comment is directed at Gio.

"Against a six it's the right move," Gio responds. He knows the game but he also knows the house wins in the long run no matter what the players do. "Maybe my split saved the table," he adds.

Thanh just shakes his head.

The next time he yells "Big Monkey," it doesn't work. I make twenty-one. As I'm taking everyone's money, Wyatt, on his way to tap out another dealer, stops and whispers in my ear: "I bet his monkey is tyyyyye-neeee." Then he pinches my ass and walks away chuckling to himself. Gio had stood up to stretch and turned toward the dice pit, so I don't think he noticed me flinch.

Before the next shoe, Gio starts flirting again, and I go along.

"When are we going to have some fun together, Traer? Grab a little dinner, split a six-pack. Or a couple bottles of wine if that's your thing."

"I'm pretty particular about what I put in my body," I say, spurring him on.

"Is that so?" He's really grinning now. "I can cook, you know. You should see what I can do with an Italian sausage."

"Ha! I'm not so sure my boyfriend would like that. You can ask him. He's on the game behind me." I motion back with my head.

"He looks like a friendly enough guy," Gio says. "I bet he wouldn't mind one bit."

We're both smiling now. It goes on like that. Meanwhile, the table turns really cold. Three times in a row Thanh yells "King Kong" and I don't bust. I can tell he's getting frustrated.

"You two should stop talking so much. Dealer slow down."

"I'm not slowing down," I say.

"Yeah. Slow down. Bad for cards."

Gio laughs. He says, "What does how fast she goes have to do with anything?"

"You not pay attention," Thanh says. I can see he's working himself up. "Split nines, no good," he explains. "Hit twelve, take dealer bust card. Not good. I know this game. Dealer talk, make mistake. Change order of cards. Pay attention. Us against dealer. We play smart, we win. Want to make friend with dealer, go other table."

"Now wait a minute," I say. He's got me worked up a bit too.

"It's all right," Gio says. He pushes back his chair and gathers his chips.

"You don't have to leave," I say.

"I was going anyway, your break's coming up," he says. "I got my money back. No thanks to Brooks Robinson over there." I don't know what he means, but he reassures me that he's leaving because it's late and that he has to get up, not because of Thanh.

"Let him go," says Thanh.

I give him a hard look. Gio leaves a ten-dollar tip and says he'll come back to see me some night soon, then he walks away, leaving just me and Thanh for a few seconds before Amanda steps up and taps me on the shoulder to go on break. She waits while I arrange my tray.

"Game go better now," Thanh says. "You see."

But I'm in no mood for it. I don't step away when the tray is in order.

"'*Game go better now,*'" I say, mocking his way of speaking. "What do I care how *game go now*? I'm the dealer. I work here. I work for tips, in case you haven't noticed. That guy you just chased away? He just happens to know more about blackjack than you'll ever know, you dumb fuck."

A switch just got flipped or something, don't ask me to explain it. Amanda heard everything.

"News flash," I go on. "Losing thousands of dollars does not make you a good gambler, it makes you an idiot. It's the middle of the night. You're here *every* night. Get a life. Go home to your family. Jesus."

Amanda taps me again, a lot harder this time, as if to say, What the hell are you doing? Get out of here before you get fired.

Finally, I go. As I'm walking to break, I'm praying Thanh won't be there when I get back, but I know that he will, he'll want to beat me, to have the last word.

I want to tell Wyatt what happened, I'm shaking I'm so mad. But he isn't in the smoking break room. I find him in the stairwell with Rachelle. She's lighting his cigarette and jumps back a little when I open the door.

"Hey, babe," Wyatt says. "How's that little monkey treating you?"

He makes a monkey sound and scratches his armpit. I don't want to tell him about it around Rachelle, so I leave them there together, laughing.

In the non-smoking break room, the only magazines are *Guns and Ammo*, *Venice '14*, and *Physics Today*. I pick up the travel guide and read the same sentence over and over. I'm having trouble focusing.

Wyatt's never going to marry me, I think to myself, looking up at the clock. It's half past one in the morning. My period is two weeks late.

Flood Plain

People said old Phineas had it coming, what with a son at home and his wife sick like that, and later the way it went down with that other kid he should have just let win and chalked up to time passing. What else people said, it being Texas, was God is watching.

I wasn't watching, I was three. Phin's story is town lore. The old-timers put the beginning at Grandpa Phin's second wife, Maddie's, sarcoidosis.

> *Sarcoidosis is a systemic disease that can affect any organ. Common symptoms are vague, such as fatigue unchanged by sleep, lack of energy, weight loss, aches and pains, arthritis, dry eyes, swelling of the knees, blurry vision, shortness of breath, a dry hacking cough or skin lesions. The cutaneous symptoms range from rashes and nodules to* erythema nodosum *or* lupus pernio.

From a medical textbook I keep in the garage, just in case. More than sarcoid, Maddie had migraines, too, and high blood pressure, and chronically sore feet. My own ailments are not as numerous but just as unforgiving: for starters, three years with a stiff neck I can't turn more than a quarter to the left, and ibuprofen, which helps about as much as leeches would, is the only fix I can get general agreement on. Turns highway merges into a monster truck rally, and the painkiller kills the liver, too, something I don't exactly require assistance with.

In Maddie's case, it took the doctors all of two years to diagnose the thing, and by then they calculated she had just one year left to live. That might have been a nice piece of information in the beginning, in my opinion; it might have given her a head start on that bucket list. To her credit, she did dive in head first once the diagnosis was arrived at, even if that bucket turned out to be filled almost exclusively with dance cards of every sun-soaked wannabe-cowboy oilman from Mineola to Joaquin. Phin's infidelity beat her by a few weeks but was not the reason she blew out quicker than the Spindletop gusher. The sickness had Maddie ready to erupt one way or the other. In the end, she showed them all: lived another forty years and made two more husbands—one of them a podiatrist, no less, although no one was exactly sure his license was legit and he wasn't just some fetishist willing to lie outright—just as miserable as Phin.

What saved Phin from careening off track completely was, near the end of Maddie's roller-coaster sick time, he stumbled by dumb chance upon a girlfriend, who just happened to be twenty years his junior, name of Galaxy. She taught art at his younger son's high school, that son being my uncle Austin, now dead. In six months, Maddie was gone and he'd moved in with the girl, and together they might have quit this whole dusty scene, except it turns out there's a force to it not all that different from gravity. It couldn't help that Galaxy was no Carmelite nun. This was the Age of Aquarius, remember, so forgive and forget. Still, she ran the gamut: Traveling salesmen. Retired bankers. Carnies. One Black guy passing through town from Grambling they say gave her a dose. A man can claim indifference to that sort of thing but the shit adds up. He gets to thinking. "Hippy" was the popular term at that time, but the older ones had no patience for fads. They called her "slut." Or worse, it being Texas. Those that could did her anyway, them being men. Grandpa knew all about it, he just claimed not to care.

"She's a free *spirit*, goddammit!" his defense to anyone who would listen. "Sock it to 'em," he might add uncertainly, committed to adopting her lingo. "Of course, now that's all done."

Of course, it was not. And no one *did* listen. Even so, after they met, they say his anger, once as permanent a part of him as his polyps, was regularly transformed into a restrained bow of his head and a forgiving smile. They put one word on it, *love*, as if that explained anything.

What was Galaxy doing there in the first place? people asked out loud. One fat guy on the street yelled it in her face. It meant no more to her than it did to Grandpa. Her students loved her. At first, she was fresh relief for Phin from his long days as a driller with a team of unlucky wildcatters. "Unlucky" is kind. "Crusaders," they called themselves, which made the most sense. Energy was their holy grail. How they met was, one Friday night, Phineas, too weary from work to even wash his hands, defeated again in his life's toil, his restless wife at home with aches or lesions or maybe *erythema nodosum* or *lupus pernio*, whatever the hell that is, goes to the concession stand at Uncle Austin's football game, daydreaming perhaps of derricks, or with ineffectual horse heads bobbing in his brain, and gets in line one behind Galaxy, who's all dolled up in a floral dress with a red ribbon in her hair. Somebody write a song! I've seen pictures, and she had a way. In no time, he'd packed up all he could into an oversized duffel bag and a couple of old suitcases, not forgetting the leather satchel and pool cue his father left him when he died and nothing else, and moved into the house Galaxy was renting. A month later, he and the team strike oil. Suddenly, it's annus mirabilis. For six months he's settled down on a regular rig praising God for his good fortune. It's only when he starts to feel real happy that the shit hits the fan.

Who are we to sit in judgment of a woman, predators that we are? The day the older boy from his school first knocked on Galaxy's door, Austin was there studying, believe it or not. Uncle Austin, the idiot son, the oops child. But even an accidental idiot could see that riding the bench at left tackle would offer no escape from this dead-end valley town, with its grave sermons and catcalling shopkeepers, from the fluvial terraces surrounding it and their stratified reminder to residents of the timeless futility of man. The boy, Lopez, was in Galaxy's class, a year ahead of Austin in school. From the bed of his El Camino, he pulled out a rolled-up sheet of butcher paper and presented it at the door while Phineas was away at an inquiry.

"Since you weren't too keen on posin', I had to go by my imagination."

The boy had talent, that's the part that got lost in all that happened after. Even through the scrim of the screen door, and half-blocked by Galaxy's nice backside, Austin could see from the couch the quality in the reclining figure unfurled: a naked woman seated in the grass in his father's new girlfriend's likeness.

"Oh, Carl," she said.

Oh Carl, indeed. Austin filled in the details when it was all over. Remembering he was there, she grinned in his direction before stepping onto the porch with Lopez and lowering her voice. Austin could pick up only a few phrases of hers—"I don't know," "That wouldn't be right, Carl," "Of course, it's lovely," "No, he's not," "Carl, I'm your teacher," "Well . . . come back Wednesday, then . . . after two"—and no more of Carl's lusty tone than a cocky progression of monosyllabic assurances.

Phineas played pool on Wednesday afternoons, his usual day off. It's a pattern he kept up even during his suspension. The inquiry concerned an explosion at the well involving a pumping jack. A man was killed, another badly injured. The well had reached its economic limit, when its production rate fails to cover operating expenses. There's a formula for it:

$$EL_{oil} = \frac{WI \; x \; LOE}{N \; RI \; [P_o + (P_g \; x \; GOR/1{,}000) \; x \; (1-T)]}$$

where EL_{oil} is a well's economic limit in barrels per month, P_o and P_g . . . Shit, I never understood the damn formula. I *should* understand it. I ended up stuck in the industry like everyone else of my kin, and then knocked up the woman who would become wife number one and couldn't get unstuck. What I do know, is when the limit is reached, the well becomes a liability and is usually abandoned, but not always. Often some oil remains, and it's tempting to postpone abandonment hoping the price will go up or some better ways of recovering it will be discovered. That's what Phin's crew was doing when the accident occurred. Word was he'd been drinking.

* * *

Even though he was no older then than I am now, Phineas invited the nickname "Old" by the shuffle in his step, the way bobbing and bent over he resembled one of his rusty derricks during his frequent coughing fits, and his leathery face from outdoor work and years of smoking creased by lines you could tow a truck with. I'm no health nut either. The sore neck I can't shake will sometimes mushroom into explosive headaches. The first movement in the morning might reveal a stiff shoulder for no reason or an itchy red splotch on some part of my body just out of arm's reach. Who knows if my more frequent passing of gas is related to diet or deterioration? No doctor does, that's for sure. My second wife, in half-sleep, will throw a pillow at me on my fifth trip to pee in the night and say, "Tyler Stark . . . what? Get your ass back in bed!"

One spring, not long after I had left college, our town was overcome by a more relentless than usual creep of gray water; and then, following its retreat, by a predictable contingent of do-gooders—bureaucrats, aid workers, men of the cloth—along with an offensive coating of thick mud. One fellow with a more direct angle called himself an energy coach and set up shop in a makeshift kiosk at the center of the reconstruction. Our town is in a flood plain. This fellow's pitch to those who paid cash was that our physical presence in the world was no more than a concrete manifestation of our emotional infirmities. "Born perfect!" he would rhapsodize with a flourish, our bodies fall apart for being "protean vessels" conforming to the traumas we suppress and store away as we age. In the wake of the tragedy, he anticipated a wide range of maladies.

And he was right! Folks came to him with inexplicable rashes, hypertension, sudden limps. He would apply hands, place magnets on their knees, and ask for focus and silence so he could adjust their energy with nothing more than his will.

"A genu-*ine* healer," old Paddy still recalls at the barbershop.

The man never returned after any of the periodic floods that washed over our town in the decades since, taking furniture and household items with them on their retreat, not to mention the occasional animal carcass or human being, and leaving behind knickknacks and organisms in various states of disrepair as if the slate-gray waters had conscious parameters for choosing. His work is nevertheless still mentioned with reverence by many of those who lived through my generation's Big One. The story of his visit is the only one that lives on like Phin's does in our communal memory.

"Cured the wife's shakes and never laid a hand on her," says Gervil, also at the barbershop.

All too late for Phin, a victim of the Really Big One. After the accident on the rig, he developed afflictions of his own, beginning with the intestines. He couldn't shoot pool for more than fifteen minutes without a trip to the toilet, a source of amusement to the regulars at Big John's. "I hope I didn't hear what I just heard," he would growl, when on his return he caught a wisp of laughter or the tail end of some unflattering exchange. More than one fight ensued. The last physical symptoms of his decline coincided with his son Austin's announcement that Galaxy and Lopez had been grinding away in Phin's absence every Wednesday afternoon.

"I seen 'em through the window, Pa. With nothin' on but what nature saw fit to give 'em."

Phin sat as motionless listening to his son as he did when he watched an opponent run a table at eight ball. Then suddenly, as if he'd been poked in the gut with the slide of his opponent's backstroke, his body accordioned in on itself and his left eye began to twitch. "You go home now and stay there," he said, once he'd straightened out. "You done good." Some variation of that twitch and contortion recurred every few hours up to and including the following Wednesday, when from a tree, and with the aid of binoculars, he took advantage of sloppily closed drapes to confirm the betrayal firsthand.

* * *

Initial inclinations toward a crime of passion—perhaps a justified double homicide—were overcome soon by his feelings for Galaxy and by the realization that he was unfit and middle-aged and the boy Lopez was a dangerous young stallion. Hints to his son of a complicated plan for bodily injury to both, then one, then the other were replaced by bouts of drinking, an afternoon of private fist-pounding, and a waterslide of self-pity that ended in a pool of resignation, settling finally on a pathetic plan for insufficient restitution: property damage of the most meager kind. As if to make up for the shabbiness of his idea—to smash up the kid's new car—he threw himself into the details. He'd do it with his son's old baseball bat, that part was simple. Where would Lopez's parents be? At work, he learned, after asking around. What about Lopez? At school, of course, if he did it on a weekday. Then why would his car be at home and not with him at school? Because Phin would punch a hole in one of the tires with an awl the night before while everyone was asleep. Wouldn't the neighbors recognize him bashing up the car? Not if he wore a mask.

Galaxy would be left unharmed despite his son's urging. "Pa, if you seen him stickin' it to her doggy style on that old leather chair, you'd be singing a different tune."

"I *seen* it!" he cried, slamming the nearest barstool. "*Damn* it, Austin. You can't go blaming a freedom-loving woman for behaving like a man." Say what you want, in many ways Phin was ahead of his time.

Of course, his grace did not extend to Lopez. In his mind, as he confessed to Austin, he imagined the boy much older, in his eighties or nineties, arthritic, unable to form full sentences, hobbled and using a cane. Phin had placed him in that position in his thoughts with a form of magic that he conceived of as vaguely Oriental. Awaiting his shot at Big John's the night after cracking up the boy's car, his mind rested not on the pool game, but on this latest conceit—on how the aging process might be accelerated or mirrored, or, if that wasn't possible, on how he might outlive the boy, which, as it turned out, he was just able to do.

"You gonna shoot or stare at your balls all night?"

His opponent, whom Phin did not know, was a large, gruff man who might have been helpful in a fight. Phin learned otherwise when the man backed into the bar after seeing the way Lopez came in, collar upturned, casing the room, accompanied by three leather-jacketed, buzz-cut allies—friends of Lopez, it was later revealed, each a year or two older than he, who fanned out around the pool tables in front and back of where Phin was seated to prevent his escape, like warriors staking out positions in the siege of a medieval castle. Phin's chair was tall, boxy, wooden, the kind made especially for pool rooms, with cues splayed out in a quiver-like pouch attached to the seat pad. He held onto his own cue and considered his options. Lopez's face as he stepped around the table opposite Phin was screened by the long, low-hanging fixture, until he bent forward into the light and put his palms on the green baize, grinning.

"You the guy banged up my El Camino?" he asked menacingly. Phin didn't answer straight off. He turned his head slowly to the left and to the right, and then carefully rotated to plot the third boy's position behind him.

Turning back, finally, he said, "If you're the kid banging my woman, then I'm the one who banged up your car."

In the time it takes for billiard balls to spread apart on a break, Lopez's ignorance that the man across from him was anything more than a vandal and a drunk, that he was, in fact, the old guy he had heard Galaxy was shacking up with, was betrayed by an involuntary slump in the boy's shoulders and a noticeable sag in his outer lips. As he straightened up to gather himself, his head disappeared behind the clunky lamp, which hung by two chains above the table, leaving in Phin's sightline only a muscular and headless young torso. Phin seized that moment to strike. Lunging, he shoved the fixture hard in the direction of Lopez's concealed face. The move was well-timed, except he underestimated the speed of a teenager's reflex. Lopez was able to turn and duck. The light struck him only at a glance, and he recovered instantly after stumbling to the floor. On his command, his accomplices moved in.

Big John and some others were eventually able to stop the pounding, but by that time they didn't have to, those boys had done all they came to do, they had no mind for killing. A bloodied lip, a sore ribcage was all, and a smeared red splotch on the green felt next to Phin, who was curled up fetal-like with his right ear suspended over a side pocket. He could've taken a minute or two more of it, easy, and the irony is, if he'd been forced to, he might not have had the energy to do what he did that followed. During the scrum to pull the boys back, he rolled onto the floor where his pool cue had fallen. He still had it in him to kneel, press to his feet, and in one motion grip the old stick and swing it hard.

The bartender clutching Lopez's jacket ducked. This time Lopez was too slow, he got clipped in the side of the head. The cue snapped, and by God's will severed an artery in the boy's neck, and then everywhere was blood. A paramedic pronounced him dead on arrival.

* * *

What happened next depends upon whom you ask. Phin got out of there, the only question is how. It might be that the boy's companions were too concerned with Lopez's condition to notice Phin stealing away. Others insist an all-out brawl took shape and created a distraction. The police came, that much is certain. Arrests were made, a full night of questions endured, a poignant phone call placed by the sheriff to Lopez's inconsolable mother. Phin missed it all. He turned rabbit quick. For two weeks the police investigated, they set up stakeouts and phone taps. Conventional wisdom said you'd never see old Phineas again.

About then the flood waters came, the biggest of all time. There was warning enough for a week of sandbagging, and the town got busy. Speculation about Phin was put on hold. The bags did no good in the end, most folks got washed out. When the river finally went back to bed, the authorities had putting things back in order on their minds, not finding Phin, whom many folks figured for being in the right anyway, so were not too keen on expending public treasure chasing after. That Mexican nailed Phin's girl, the chorus went; he deserved what he got. So, between the mud and the morals, the missing man was forgotten, which is why it came as such a surprise when he was the only one in town who turned up dead, surrounded by weeds in a gulley with rigor mortis set in. An arbitrary cluster of items had settled near him in the muck, most likely washed in from the neighboring junkyard: a seed spreader, a Batman costume, an old cast-iron tub. A soaked love letter discovered in his shirt pocket was rimmed with hearts. The ink was too runny to reveal his last words except one: Galaxy.

We are all going to die. Maybe not that messily, but close enough to it. Say it one hundred times and it starts to sink in. Die! Die! Die! Forty-three hundred inhabitants survive a five-hundred-year flood, and the only one who drowns is the one they all calculated was long gone. Figure it all out and tell me when you do. It's a roulette wheel! To me, every one of them underestimated what Galaxy made Phineas remember, that life is not all digging and decay. Why else would a grown man near fifty be sleeping under a bridge when all the world can see he's got but two choices: get the hell out of town or turn yourself in and roll the dice on the law, God, and Texas? Well, God and Texas were never on his side, but the law can be flexible. There's the unwritten code, to begin with, as well as self-defense. The whole business, when you think about it, reeks of self-defense: the drilling, the drinking, the swinging lamp, the teenage lover, the tales about a visiting shaman. Hell, even the foot doctor. Not to mention Phin's love for Galaxy (a better word might be *yearning*). The sandbags, too. And the way everyone in town hangs on to Phin's story like it's a cliff or a ledge and they're the hero, for having survived, at the end of some third-rate action adventure. Just give us our goddamn youth back! Even the headaches and the incontinence must be some kind of self-defense. You name it. It all is.

Acknowledgments

Gratefully acknowledged are the following journals, where many of the stories here previously appeared:

2 Bridges Review ("Rabbit")
Valparaiso Fiction Review ("Shih Tzu" and "Skinny Dugan")
Midwestern Gothic ("Psychiatrist")
The Prague Revue ("Scripts")
West Trade Review ("Tennessee")
The Doctor T.J. Eckleburg Review ("Government")
The Nassau Review ("King Kong")
Poydras Review ("Flood Plain")
Tartts Fiction 8 (reprint of "Shih Tzu")

I would also like to express my gratitude to the staff at Cornerstone Press, especially to Dr. Ross Tangedal, the publisher; Brett Hill, the editorial director; Maria Scherer, the managing editor; and Julia Kaufman, the production editor; who, along with their teams, patiently and expertly carved a recognizable form out of the rough block of stone that I originally provided them.

Work of this nature would be next to impossible without solid family support. In that I have been fortunate. My loving mom and dad, Carol Schorsch and Lou Mertes, have backed me at every turn, including the many hairpins. Nicole Mertes, my stepmother, has offered nothing but encouragement. My sister Stacey is a model of bravery, generosity, humor, and resilience, who brings light to everyone she meets, no one more so than I. And my wife and kids—well, what can you say? Their kindness and strength and love are the rock that I stand on.

Certain old and new friends are also deserving of thanks, each of whom taught me something invaluable about the human spirit. I am referring to Jessica Beever, Jill Cockson, and Sheri Parr; to Scott Kosar for his outsized role in the early Wild Years; to Jeremy Schmidt and Dan Stevens, men to the last; to Laure Brost for her infectious laughter; and to Courtney Fletcher, whose inexhaustible good cheer was a beacon to me for so long. To all: thank you.

Finally, a shout-out to the Chicago boys for their enduring friendship. You know who you are and how much it means.

COREY MERTES received his bachelor's degree from the University of Chicago and a Master of Fine Arts in Film and Television Production from the University of Southern California. After USC, he taught ballroom dance and worked in casinos as a dice dealer and a pit boss before becoming a lawyer. His short stories have appeared in many journals and have been shortlisted for the Tartts Fiction Award, the American Fiction Short Story Award, and the Hudson Prize. This is his first collection.